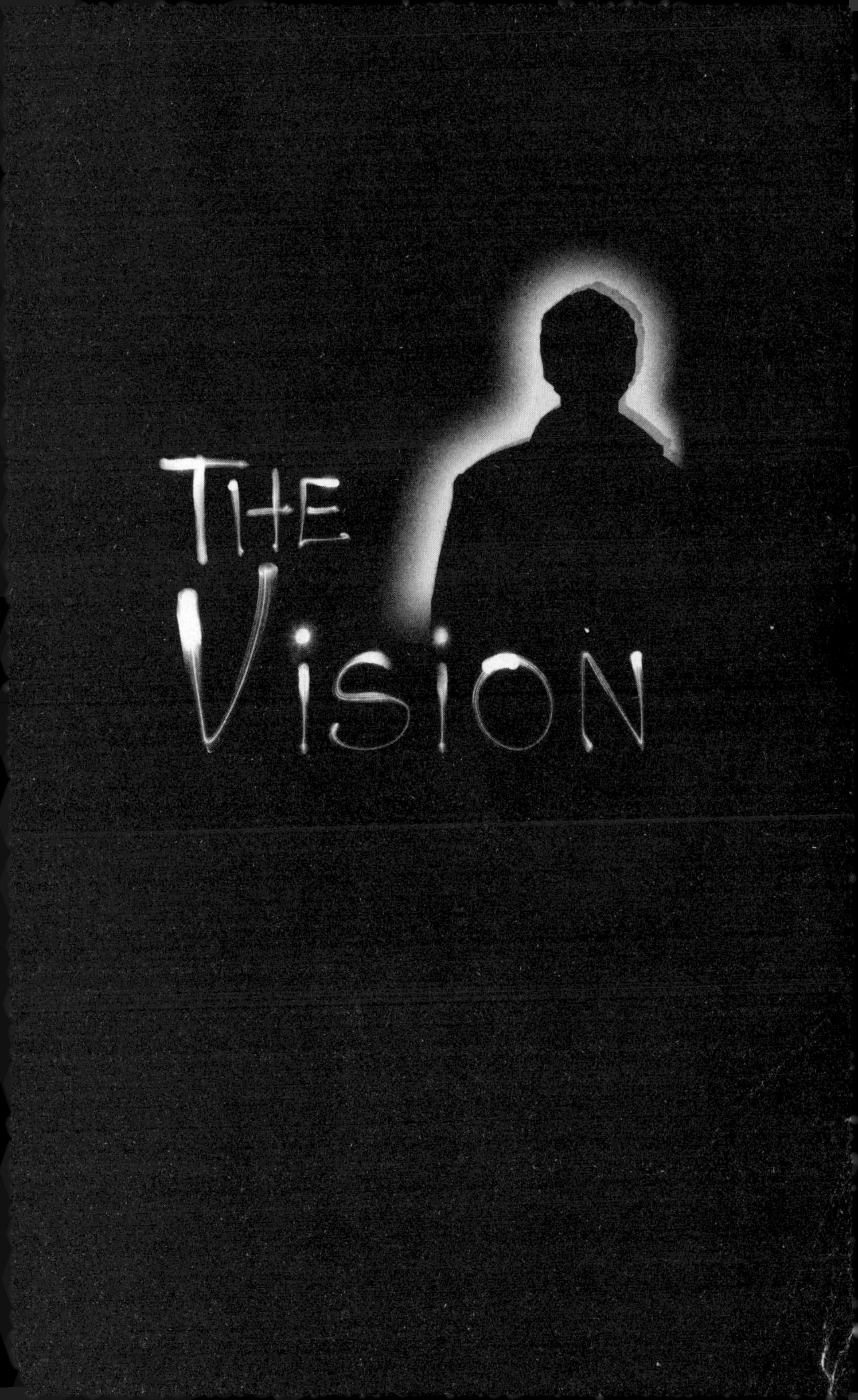
THE VISION

ALSO BY JEN NADOL

The Mark

THE VISION

JEN NADOL

BLOOMSBURY

NEW YORK BERLIN LONDON SYDNEY

First published in the United States of America in September 2011
by Bloomsbury Books for Young Readers
www.bloomsburyteens.com

For information about permission to reproduce selections from this book, write to
Permissions, Bloomsbury BFYR, 175 Fifth Avenue, New York, New York 10010

Library of Congress Cataloging-in-Publication Data
Nadol, Jen.
The vision / by Jen Nadol. — 1st U.S. ed.
p.   cm.
Sequel to: The mark.
Summary: Seventeen-year-old Cassie, now working in a funeral home on the outskirts of Chicago,
continues to try to learn about death and her ability to identify people who will soon die, but her
efforts to get help from others like herself only prove that she is on her own.
ISBN 978-1-59990-597-6
[1. Psychic ability—Fiction.   2. Death—Fiction.   3. Fate and fatalism—Fiction.   4. Under-
takers and undertaking—Fiction.   5. Orphans—Fiction.   6. Illinois—Fiction.]   I. Title.
PZ7.N13353Vis 2011   [Fic]—dc22   2011004927

Book design by Regina Roff
Typeset by Westchester Book Composition
Printed in the U.S.A. by Quad/Graphics, Fairfield, Pennsylvania
2 4 6 8 10 9 7 5 3 1

for Joe
because no moon is an island

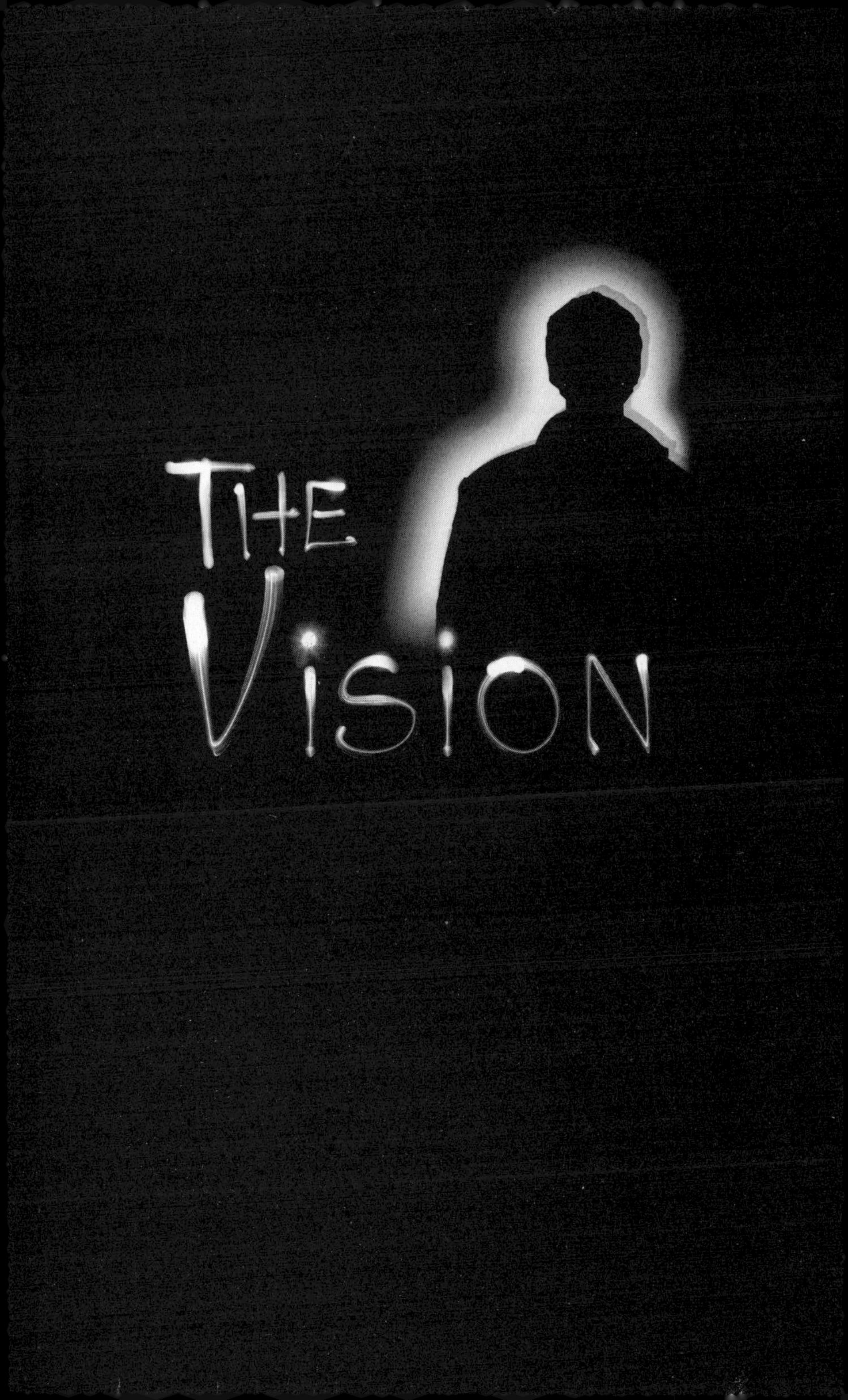
THE VISION

The man on the gurney looked just like Mr. Dempsey, my history teacher back in Ashville, Pennsylvania. He had the same scraggly Abe Lincoln beard, the same bushy eyebrows, even the same too-big ears. His nose was different, but I knew it wasn't *actually* my history teacher anyway, because I was in Illinois, not Pennsylvania, and this guy had come in with papers that said his name was James Killiam.

I'd never seen James Killiam before, hadn't followed him through rainy streets—the mark making him easy to track—or watched him sitting on a bench one bitter afternoon, like I had Walter Ness. I had nothing to do with his being here, which made what I was doing less uncomfortable. Though it was still weird being this close to him, partly because he looked so much like Mr. Dempsey, but mostly because he was naked. And dead.

"Cassie? Are you going to start the cleaning?"

I blinked, shook my head. "Sorry. Zoning."

Mr. Ludwig handed me the soapy sponge to wipe down the body, guiding as I worked. "Don't press too hard, you don't want to tear the skin. That's good. That part'll be covered by clothes so it doesn't have to be sparkling. No one's going to eat off him, you know." He smiled and winked.

Funeral home humor is weak. At best.

James Killiam was the first body Mr. Ludwig actually had me work on, though I'd watched plenty. Eleven to be exact. Enough to know the first steps by heart: match the toe tag to the papers, check for a pulse, look at the eyes. Corneas cloud over when someone's dead, and you want to be darn sure they are before doing the stuff we do here at Ludwig & Wilton.

"I think you've got it, Cassie. That's great!" Mr. Ludwig beamed, his eyes crinkling slightly, the only visible wrinkles on his smooth Japanese skin. He stepped back after I'd swabbed from neck to toe. "I guess you're finished for today. You're welcome to stay and watch the embalming . . ."

I glanced at my watch, trying to erase the feel of clammy flesh. It was already past seven, my shift officially over eight minutes ago. I shook my head. "Not tonight," I said. "Lots of homework. See you Saturday?"

He nodded, bending close to the body to slip in eye caps as I headed for the locker room.

I tossed my scrubs in the biohazard bin, then washed and rewashed my hands, still smelling like a science experiment as I pulled a hoodie over my T-shirt and jeans. At the door I slipped on Nan's old wool coat—now mine—and yanked my long, dark ponytail free before buttoning up. Then I hoisted my backpack, called good-bye to Mr. Ludwig, and walked to the bus stop a block away.

It was dark out and ice cold as I stood by the metal signpost, wondering aimlessly if your tongue would really freeze to it and eyeing the warm glow of Ludwig & Wilton's lights enviously.

I'd started there almost three months ago, a few weeks after moving to Bellevue, which wasn't a bad place. It had a decent town center and was only a short El ride to Chicago. Still, I missed home.

I missed my friends and school and teachers. I missed the mocha lattes at my favorite coffee shop. I especially missed Jack.

But I couldn't have stayed.

The bus swung wide around the corner, rolling toward me through leftover snow. I climbed aboard, blowing on mittened hands as I sat.

It had taken a while to convince Mr. Ludwig to hire me. People don't usually beat down the door to work at a funeral parlor, I guess. And if they do, they're probably not normal. Or seventeen. Or girls.

But I'm not exactly a normal seventeen-year-old girl either. And I wasn't working there for spending money or just some after-school job.

I was doing it because I need to understand death.

Not just in some hazy philosophical way, but physically, spiritually, emotionally. Any way I can. So that maybe I'll know what to do the next time I see someone like Walter Ness.

It was two weeks ago when I passed him on my way to Wicker Park with Liv. I trotted behind her down the frigid sidewalks toward a new thrift store she'd read about in the *Trib*. My head was bent, mouth and nose tucked into my scarf, and I was thinking how much I wished it was May instead of February, even though I've never seen May in Chicago and it could be just as horribly frozen and slushy as it's been the whole time I've lived here and wondering why I didn't have a good pair of snow—or at least rain—boots, when the unnatural light caught my eye.

It's funny how the limbic system, or whatever controls your emotions, works separately from the thinking brain, because a wave of nervous fear rolled through me immediately before I consciously understood that I'd looked because of the light. It was soft like a candle, in a place where there should be none—no glow cast from a store or ray of sun on this gray and gloomy day. My body recognized it instantly. The mark.

I slowed, grinding to a stop like a machine just unplugged, as I studied the man on the bench across the street. He was old, sitting motionless beside a newspaper that fluttered loosely in the wind. A dark overcoat that didn't look nearly warm enough fell in wrinkles around him, and he wore a newsboy cap, faded on the left center brim where he gripped to put it on. For a second I thought he might be asleep, but then he shifted, just slightly, maybe feeling my gaze, and I saw hollowness under his eyes. And the pallor of his skin. Like the colors of death I saw at the funeral home were already taking over.

My throat felt tight, the way it gets every time, and I couldn't move. Even though it was rude to stare. Even though Liv was now half a block ahead. Even though I wanted nothing more than to be away from this man with the mark that meant he'd die before the day was over.

Tell him or don't? Save him or not?

Trade another life for his?

Liv was almost a full block away when I finally moved, barely conscious I was doing so. I went to the man and started talking, words tumbling out, telling him he was in danger, I had a gift, could sometimes see when someone might die. He just stared. I heard my voice wavering, but I kept on, hating every awful, nervous, guilty instant of telling this terrible secret, second-guessing myself the whole time, fearful of what I might change. Or not.

I finished talking and stood breathlessly before him, my mind racing back over what I'd said.

The man was silent for a few seconds, then said simply, "Thank you for the warning."

I waited, but he didn't get up. My stomach sank. "Do you need help to stand?"

"No."

"Well, don't you want to go inside? Somewhere warm? Maybe . . . see a doctor?"

"Young lady," he said tiredly. "I'm eighty-six years old. My wife died seventeen years ago, God rest her soul. My son lives in Japan. I see him once a year, if I'm lucky. My body aches most mornings and it's a good day if I can go to the bathroom without a problem. If today's my day, so be it. I'm ready."

It was exactly like what my grandmother Nan said when I'd warned her. Exactly what I knew in my gut as I stood across the street watching him, hesitating because I knew I shouldn't tell. But I'd done it anyway.

"Did you know you might die today?" I asked too aggressively. I could see Liv coming toward us and I was angry at myself. He looked sick—*deathly*, if I was honest about it—much more than anyone I'd ever told. He'd had his time.

"Any of us might die any day," he said without drama. "You included."

Liv reached us then, thankfully too late to hear anything. She punched my shoulder lightly, raising an eyebrow. "What gives, Renfield?"

I steered her away, mumbling something about mistaking him for a friend from home.

"Who?" she asked, glancing back at him. "He's like a hundred years old."

I followed Liv the final few blocks to the thrift store, where she got some plaid pants and a leather jacket that looks really cool on her. I'd have found it first if I'd been *seeing* the clothes I flipped through instead of that man, outlined in the soft glow of the mark. What if he took my advice? Decided to go to a doctor after all? It nauseated me to realize I was hoping he wouldn't. I was wishing him dead.

All because of a few sentences in an old letter I had little reason to believe. Clearly, *didn't* believe or I'd never have warned him.

Would I?

This is why I need to understand death.

And this is why I'd come to Bellevue, far from home, much bigger and, above all, populated with an unusually strong minority of Greeks.

Some of them would have been able to read the original letter in the book Nan gave me almost two years ago. I didn't need them to translate, though. That was already done. I needed answers about what it said.

Am I really Fate?

Does saving one person condemn another?

Are there others like me?

chapter 2

"Luuucy, I'm home," I called, hanging my school bag on a hook by the door and catching a whiff of chemicals. Eau de Manicured Dead.

Petra was hunched over a bunch of psych files at our antique dining table, one of the few things she'd brought from her place in Kansas. We'd bought mismatched chairs at a yard sale down the street and painted them red. They looked funky and cool in our otherwise boring apartment.

"How was it today?" she asked.

"Okay." I shrugged off my coat, then sat to untie my wet Converse. They'd gotten soaked in the slushy walk from Ludwig & Wilton to the bus stop. I really needed boots. "You?"

"About the same."

"Whatcha working on?" I crossed, barefoot, to the fridge.

"Ugh. Floor round-up for the staff meeting tomorrow. There's so much here . . ." Over the bar counter of the kitchen I saw her wave at the papers spread everywhere. Petra shook her head.

"I can't even find time to organize my notes, much less figure out how to help these people."

I nodded, having heard it before. Pretty much every week since she'd started at Vauxhall Mental Hospital. I worried she might regret moving, maybe enough to do an about-face. But when I finally had the courage to bring it up, Petra had dismissed it immediately. "What would I go back to?" she asked. "School's done, couldn't find a job, dumped the boyfriend . . ." She'd ticked off each on her black-painted fingernails. "I feel so *needed* here."

She was talking about Vauxhall, but also about me.

I wandered closer to the table, soda in hand. Petra glanced at me, her dark bangs sticking up where she'd been resting her hand. Or pulling out her hair.

"Want to take a crack at it?" she offered.

"Uh, not in a million years?"

"It's not *that* bad."

"Mm-hmm. If you say so."

Petra went back to her notes and I flopped onto the couch, typing a quick text to Jack: "lots of homework 2nite. procrastinating. how r u?" I tried calling Tasha, too, but her phone was off. Sleeping, I realized. It was almost three a.m. in Romania, where she was spending the semester. I could never get the time difference right. And I knew Liv was out for her dad's birthday, which left me with nothing but schoolwork and laundry.

I was about to head to my room to start one or the other, when Petra said, "Hey, we got an admission this week you might be interested in."

"Really?" I sounded casual, but my stomach felt like the floor had just dropped out. There was only one thing Petra could be talking about.

"Greek girl, eighteen. Attempted suicide."

"Yeeeaah . . . ?" A lot like my mother, but I could tell there was more.

"Her parents said she was having visions before her attempt."

"What kind of visions?"

Petra paused and I could feel my heartbeat, fast and hard, all the way to my eardrums. "She said she saw death."

Oh. My. God.

I'd been waiting for this, but only in the way you wait for a call saying you've won the lottery or been chosen homecoming queen—something on the barest fringes of possible. I half expected Petra might forget to watch for a patient like my mom. So I could learn what kind of person she had been, I'd said, this mother I never knew.

But I hadn't really thought it would happen. What was the likelihood there would ever be one?

Except there was.

I leaned back slowly, not even sure what I was feeling. Shock, for sure. Elation, maybe? A weird euphoria that I might actually have found someone like her. Like me.

And fear. Definitely fear, because it meant this might all be real.

Petra nodded sympathetically. "It's a little spooky how much she sounds like your mom, right?'

"It is." I paused, playing the question in my head first to be sure I wasn't giving anything away. "What did she mean about seeing death? Did she say how?" My mom's psych file, which Petra read to me back in Kansas, had no details, so she couldn't make a comparison. But I could.

"Her parents were pretty emotional when they spoke to the doctor," Petra said. "They didn't give specifics, just said she'd been depressed, progressively more so. Talked about being surrounded by death, even said—and I quote—'the angel of death is lurking.' Poetic, huh?"

It wasn't how I'd put it, but the mark *did* look angelic if you didn't know what it meant. In fact, I'd thought that very thing when I'd seen it on my ex, Lucas. Until the truth sank in.

"She alternated between withdrawal and bursts of excitement for a couple of weeks. Classic manic-depressive," Petra said. "And then she slit her wrists."

"Ugh." I was silent, chilled by the bluntness of it—the statement and the act—and working up the courage to ask, "Can I come see her?"

Petra shrugged. "Sure. But you know you can't tell anyone what I've told you."

"Of course."

"Visiting hours are four to seven. I checked her schedule and she'll be around," Petra said. "No therapy or anything."

"Okay," I said, feeling like I was literally pushing the words out. "I'll come by after school."

I moved here specifically for this, I told myself. To find someone like me who might know things about the mark and what I was supposed to do with it. But facing the possibility that maybe I *had* made me queasy. Did I really want to hear the things this girl might tell me?

"No Corpse Central tomorrow?" Petra asked.

I shook my head. "Not till Saturday. We've got a viewing."

"Mmm. Delicious." Petra licked her lips, grinning. She was alternately repulsed and fascinated by my job. Of course, so was I.

"Has anyone else been to see her?" I asked.

"Not sure," said Petra. "I haven't actually seen her myself. She was admitted last Tuesday and was in therapy when I had rounds yesterday. Want me to check?"

"Nah." Not yet. Not until I confirm she's what I think she is—a descendant of the Fates like the women of my family, all dead now. "I'll just stop by, see what she's all about."

Petra nodded. "I think it'll be good for you, Cass. Not that you're not okay, but closure is good for all of us."

"Right." Except this was nearly the opposite of closure. It was like nudging a door sitting quietly ajar just to see what was in there.

chapter 3

I sat in English by myself. Just like I sat in computers and Spanish and history. I was still getting used to the size of Franklin Parris High School. There were almost three hundred kids in my junior class. I'd made friends with three of them.

I started right after Thanksgiving break, eating lunch alone at one end of a long table each day. I kept my head down, pushing food into random patterns, and thinking about my small school in Ashville. About lunches with Tasha, who'd taught us geography via foreign curse words, and Jack, whose fingers laced through mine made me hate the two hours and fifty minutes separating us from another lazy afternoon together.

Not that it would have been like that anymore. Or could have been. I needed anonymity. But it sucked being *this* alone.

On Friday of my first week, a girl with a white-blond ponytail caught up to me after chemistry on my dreadful walk to the cafeteria.

"How'd you do on the quiz?" she asked.

"Not good." It had been a surprise, to see if we were "on our toes." I wasn't.

"Yeah, me either," she said. "Not my best subject."

"Right. Mine either." I glanced over. She was tall. Most people are to me, but this girl was at least five eight or nine. She had smooth, pale skin and almost colorless hair. Fluorescent light sparkled off rhinestones on her black cat's-eye glasses. I looked away so she wouldn't catch me staring and know how desperate I was for company. I'd never had to *make* friends in Ashville, having gone to school with the same kids for as long as I could remember.

"I'm Liv," she said, rescuing me.

"Cassie," I answered.

"Yeah, I know. You're new." We'd reached the lunchroom by then. I hesitated, scanning the crowd as if for friends. "Come sit with us," Liv invited, adding with a wry smirk, "Unless you like sitting alone."

I followed her to the food line and loaded my tray with spaghetti, Cheetos, and chocolate milk, hoping we'd have something to talk about once we sat. Liv turned, surveying my choices. "FYI," she said, "Hannah and Erin are gonna tell you that's gross."

"What?" I studied my lunch. I loved Cheetos. And chocolate milk. As far as I was concerned they went with whatever was on the menu. But I could see how Hannah or Erin—whoever they were—might not agree. I checked Liv's tray. "But"—I looked at her, confused—"you have the same stuff."

"Yup." She winked. "That's how I know what they'll say."

She led me to a table near the middle of the cafeteria where two girls were hunched over half-slips of paper.

"Ugh," Liv said, plunking her bag beside them. "You are *not* talking about the PSATs."

The redhead looked up, freckles dusting her button nose. "Did you get yours?"

"Of course," Liv said. "They sucked."

The girl winced and bit her lip. "Sorry, Liv."

Liv shrugged, waved it away. "Whatevs." She gestured for me to take a seat. "This is Cassie. She's new. From . . ."

"Pennsylvania," I said.

"Pennsylvania," Liv repeated. "Cassie, this is Erin . . ." She pointed at the redhead, who smiled. "And Hannah."

"Hey," the other girl said, twisting her dark, wavy hair into a thick spiral and eyeing my tray. "Did Liv make you get that?"

"Yup." I nodded. "She said it's what all the cool kids eat."

Liv snorted.

"I'm just kidding." Sarcasm might be more welcome later, I realized. After Hannah decided whether she liked me. I smiled and shrugged. "I guess we just have the same weird taste."

Erin reached across the table for Hannah's PSAT scores and slid them above hers for comparison.

"So how bad were they?" she asked Liv.

"My parents," Liv said, meatball paused midair, "are going to completely *freak*."

"Maybe you don't tell them?" Hannah offered.

"As if they haven't been asking every day if I've gotten them?"

"Yeah," Hannah agreed. She looked at me, her blue eyes framed dramatically with dark shadow. "Are your parents as crazy about stuff like this as Liv's and Erin's?"

"No." I hesitated. Here comes the conversation killer. "Actually, my parents died when I was little. I live with a friend."

All three of them stared at me. I waited for the questions—*what kind of friend? how'd they die? where's the rest of your family?* Or worse, the awkward silence.

Liv was the first to speak. "Well, can I trade lives with you for the rest of the year?"

I might have hugged her if I'd known her for more than ten minutes. "The PSATs are just practice, you know," I said, indescribably relieved to talk about something normal. "They don't actually count for anything."

"They count for National Merit," Erin piped up.

Liv rolled her eyes. "If you're a genius." She popped a Cheeto in her mouth, talking while she chewed but somehow avoiding being gross. "Yeah, I know they don't count for anything. Except in my house. There will be *hours* of discussion about 'good schools'"— Liv framed the word with finger quotes—"and 'my future.'" More quotes. "I'm not sure what kind of 'discussion' it is since I never get to talk." She kept her bent fingers up after that last one for emphasis.

"It's really more like a monologue," Hannah said.

"Or soliloquy," Erin added.

"That's why you got a sixty-eight on verbal," Hannah told Erin, who beamed.

"Either way," Liv said, hands in her lap now, "what *I* want isn't up for discussion."

"And what you want is . . . ?" I asked.

"Oh, who knows?" She sighed. "Art school? Maybe? It's the only class I'm any good at." She frowned. "What I *really* want is just not to have to think about it so freakin' much."

"Well . . . what's wrong with art school?" I asked.

"*They call them starving artists for a reason*," Liv said snippily, obviously mimicking a parent.

"You don't have to be a *fine* artist," I said. "I'll bet there are lots of jobs you could do with an art degree."

"Maybe you can tell that to my parents," she said. "'Cause they sure won't listen to me."

The conversation turned to less contentious stuff after that—
what Erin should wear to her MIT interview, which Hollywood
stars Hannah was crushing on. I mostly listened, clueless about
both.

Liv waited until lunch was over that day, Hannah and Erin near
the hallway sorting their trash, to nudge my arm. When I looked
up, she nodded toward a table a few rows down with a raised eyebrow and sly smile.

"He's smokin' hot, right?"

"Huh?"

Liv rolled her eyes. "Puh-leeze, Cassie. Don't think I didn't
see you looking. You've barely taken your eyes off him all period."

It wasn't true. Not really. Though I had been watching the
table of kids. Not only at lunch, but in the hallways around school.
I'd noticed them my very first day, their dark hair and distinctive
features strikingly similar to mine. They were just who I was
looking for. Greeks. And I knew exactly which one she was talking
about. "Who is he?"

"Zander Dasios, but don't even think about it," Liv said firmly.
"He's a total player. You want no part of that."

Zander. I weighed the name, something about its unique
sharpness fitting him perfectly. His hair was lush, wavy, and disheveled, long enough that he could just tuck a piece behind his ear,
only to have it slip forward again. He had a way of looking out
from behind that fallen hair to catch you staring and smirk, his
eyes saying that he'd known you were watching all along.

"I wasn't looking at him anyway," I told Liv, picking up my
tray and walking toward the trash can.

"Uh-huh."

That was three months ago. Liv, Hannah, Erin, and I had sat

at our same table every day since, and the Greeks sat at theirs. I had no clue how to approach them, so I studied them instead, looking for an opening.

Petra had found me something much better in the girl at the hospital, though I was dreading my visit today. Even more so when I saw Liv by my locker after English, bouncing from one foot to the other, full of her usual excess energy. "Only six more classes and we're off to Chi-town!" she sang as I approached.

Shit. I'd totally forgotten we were supposed to go shopping. And, yes, I was still going to the city, but there's no way I could bring Liv along to see Demetria Kansokis.

She read it on my face. "Uh-oh, what is it, Renfield? You look like your cat died."

"I don't have a cat."

"Not anymore," she said cheerfully.

"I'm sorry, Liv." Which was true. "But I can't do the vintage stores today. I've gotta meet Petra at the hospital."

Liv turned serious. "Is she okay?"

"Completely. The hospital she works at, not one she's been admitted to."

"Oh. Okay. So what's up?"

"Nothing major," I said, ad libbing an excuse. "Just some paperwork for our lease. Our landlord is doing something financial with the property, needs us to come sign some stuff . . ." It was a lame excuse, but I could see Liv's eyes glaze at the word "financial," like I'd hoped they would.

"Well, that sucks," she said. "Can't you just sign the stuff and then go?"

I shook my head. "I wish I could, but Petra isn't sure how long it'll take and we can't risk losing the place . . ." I let it dangle, hoping the reminder of my unusual and tenuous—at least compared to Liv's—living situation would be enough to hold off more questions. It was.

"Oh, all right." Liv sighed, rolling her eyes. "Maybe I'll see if Erin or Hannah want to go instead."

"Yeah," I said, feeling a twinge that I'd miss out. "That's a good idea."

She scouted the hall, then leaned close, whispering conspiratorially, "But Hannah's mom won't let her wear 'used clothing' and Erin's a sweetie, but she just has"—she did another melodramatic visual sweep—"bad taste." Liv clapped a hand over her mouth and gave me an exaggerated wink. "I like shopping with you better."

I couldn't help smiling, though the reminder of how I'd be spending my afternoon instead made my stomach churn. I nodded sagely and stage-whispered back, "It'll be our secret."

chapter 4

The El was nearly empty, rush-hour riders going in the opposite direction. I grabbed a seat at the back of the car and flipped open my history book, but after reading the same sentence about James Madison for the third time, I gave up and looked out the window instead. Houses, shops, and streets slid by, faster and faster as we accelerated toward the city. Dusk had fallen and everything was tinged with the crisp, bluish hue of winter, harsher than I remembered it being at home. Jack would be at basketball practice now. Sometimes afterwards he'd come to my apartment or find me in the library, wrapping his freshly showered body around me from behind, wet hair teasing my ear, his cheek scratchy against mine.

I wondered what he did these days.

I knew his phone would be tucked in his backpack, hanging in the locker room, but I texted anyway, the connection making it feel like a small part of him was here, keeping me company: "freezing today, but going to chicago anyway. how r u?"

Twenty minutes later—far too soon—I was there.

* * *

I trotted the block to Vauxhall Hospital, slowing only as I slipped into the warmth of the lobby and that too-familiar hospital smell. I wound through the maze of corridors and stairwells, stopping at the swinging doors of Demetria's ward to mentally rehearse the lines Petra had coached me on: I was a friend from school, Demetria and I sat next to each other in history class.

"They won't ask you to prove it and unless Demetria refuses to see you, you'll get in," Petra had said. "We like to encourage patients to interact with familiar faces from the outside world."

"But what if she does? Refuse, I mean?"

Petra shrugged. "Then you leave. But I don't think that'll happen. She's been pretty unresponsive to just about everything from what I heard." Petra paused, then added, "If you see you're upsetting her, though, you've gotta get a nurse involved. Especially since we're on ground that's a little shaky, ethically speaking. After all, you're *not* a school friend *or* a familiar face."

Petra was silent and I could almost see her rethinking this plan. I jumped in before she could change her mind.

"I'll be careful. Really, Petra, I promise. And if she gets worked up, I'll get someone."

"I trust you, Cass, which is the only reason I'm going along with this," she said, still hesitant. "The more I think about it, the less kosher it seems, but I think you're sensitive to the situation. And visiting this girl might do you *and* her some good. An unfamiliar face might actually be more help." She shook her finger at me, only half teasing. "But I'm counting on you to do the right thing if you see it's not."

So it was with all that in mind that I approached the nurses' station, worried I'd be tossed out on my butt before I even got to see her. But the nurse gave me only a cursory glance, inspected my bookbag, had me fill out the visitor log, and checked my ID.

I was in.

Demetria Kansokis was sitting on a scratchy-looking sofa, the TV blaring from its shelf overhead. They were never down low, Petra said. Safety reasons. Demetria was staring past it anyway, her dark hair long like mine, hanging in thick, scraggly waves. It looked like she might have showered last week. I didn't blame her, though. Who knew what she'd seen that brought her here.

My heart beat faster as I approached, a nervous rhythm that felt almost visible. I wasn't sure what to say and didn't know what I wanted more: for her to admit she was Fate or have no idea what I was talking about.

There were three other patients on the sofas and chairs nearby. One of them looked up at me expectantly.

"Nurse?" he said.

"Um, no." I was wearing a gray jersey dress and every person I'd seen in the hospital so far was head-to-toe white. But crazy people have their own reality. Actually, I think that's the definition of crazy.

"Do you have my medication?"

"I'm not a nurse."

"You look like a nurse."

No. I don't. Not even a little bit. "Well, I'm not. I'm just visiting."

"Do you have my medication?"

"No."

He turned back to the TV and I glanced at Demetria. She and the other two patients seemed like they hadn't even heard our conversation. As if they weren't even in the same room with us, really. Maybe they'd had his medication.

As I slid into a chair, her eyes flicked in my direction, then immediately returned to a spot left of the TV.

"Demetria?"

No response.

"Are you Demetria Kansokis?"

Still nothing. I glanced around the room again, feeling stupid and uncomfortable, but no one was paying any attention to me. Even the nurse by the door was more interested in her magazine. Resolutely, I turned back to the girl.

"My name's Cassie. Cassandra Renfield. That's my father's last name," I added. "My mother's was Dinakis." I waited to see if that made any impression, but it was as if I were invisible. And inaudible.

"I thought you might like some company," I said.

"She can't hear you," Medicine Man offered without looking at me.

"I think she can."

"Nuh-uh."

I ignored him. "I know you can hear me," I told her. "You don't have to talk if you don't want to. I just thought if you *did* want to . . . you know, talk to someone who's not part of the hospital or anything . . ." I trailed off, realizing this was ridiculous. Petra said she hadn't been talking in her sessions. Why on earth would she talk to me? But I didn't know what else to do.

"I just moved here a couple months ago, after my grandmother died," I said, thinking it might have helped to have rehearsed *this* part more and the nurses'-station part less. "My parents died a long time ago, so Nan was my only real family. I miss her a lot and thought being somewhere different might help."

Demetria shifted slightly in her seat, but still didn't speak. Or even look at me.

"I don't know a lot of people here," I rambled on. "I've made a few friends, but I'd really hoped to meet some other Greeks. Nan never told me much about our people and I was kind of hoping to learn. There's a bunch of Greek kids at my school, but I'm not sure how to, you know, get in with them."

"Why don't you offer them some peanuts?"

Great idea, Medicine Man. I'll get right on that. "I'm not sure they like peanuts," I said out loud.

"I love peanuts."

"Uh-huh."

"They don't let me have them here." He leaned over, close enough to whisper. I could smell his breath, hot and antiseptic. "They interfere with my medication."

"Right."

I shifted, subtly inching farther from Medicine Man, and glanced at the door, looking for someone who might distract him or, even better, take him away. Instead, I saw a flash of dark, tousled hair. A guy passing just out of sight. He looked like Zander Dasios, who'd been leaning lazily against the wall of lockers around the corner from mine as I'd left school, an image that lingered teasingly in my subconscious. I rubbed my brow. Trouble. Liv was right. I'd asked Erin and Hannah and a few people in my classes about him, too. Casually, of course, in a learning-about-my-new-school way. I'd heard all the rumors: how many girls he'd gone through, how he'd stood up his prom date at another school, can't be trusted, paternity tests, drugs. Everything. Still, I couldn't get him off my mind. Even though we'd never spoken. Even though our eye contact had been only the most fleeting of looks, with me always turning away first.

I shook my head and turned back to Demetria, knowing by her stony silence that if I was going to learn anything from her, it wouldn't be today. "It's been nice visiting with you," I said. "I'd like to come back in a couple days. If you don't want me to, just say so." I smiled at my own joke—the kind of thing that'd give Petra a laugh—but then, feeling mean, added, "Really, it helps me to come. Thanks for . . . listening."

She hadn't really listened, not "actively" as my new principal liked to call it, but you never know where even a one-sided conversation might lead.

chapter 5

They arrived at the funeral home together, his wife, two daughters, one son, each clutching a little pack of tissues. I could tell from their faces that the Killiams had gone through plenty already.

His portrait was at the chapel entrance, James Killiam smiling broadly at his grieving family. He didn't quite look like that anymore. I wondered if they'd puzzle over the weirdness of it throughout the wake, like Mr. Ludwig said the family always did. After we've sewn the lips shut, plumped up the sunken face with cotton, and lathered industrial makeup on skin now naturally gray, the dead person looked like a strange replica of himself. Maybe it was better. Not quite real might be easier to let go.

James Killiam had been a cardiac doctor at a local hospital, married for twenty-eight years, devoted father, weekends at the food bank. Mr. Nice Guy. I learned it all from his funeral program, filled with the photos and highlights of his life.

The lowlights never made it in there, of course. I learned *that* from Number Four, the woman who'd done three years for drug possession. We'd dressed her in long sleeves to hide the track marks. Her program only talked about how she'd loved her daughter, always remembered her parents' birthdays. I'd found all the other stuff online, researching her just as I had each of the others I'd worked on.

If James Killiam had secrets, they weren't newsworthy.

"Spying on the party again?"

I spun around, startled. Ryan had a way of sneaking up on you. Actually, everyone here did, their mannerisms muted from years of being unobtrusive. He smiled down at me, his deep-set green eyes creasing at the corners. Nan would have called them bedroom eyes. And they would have been on someone less wholesome. Like Zander Dasios.

I closed the supply-room door, reluctantly leaving the Killiams. Ryan had caught me peeking too often already.

"Just trying to get a read on how many are here," I said. "So I can figure clean-up time and all, you know?"

"Uh-huh." He smirked. Ryan thought I was nosy, which was true, though he couldn't possibly guess the reason why.

"Shouldn't you be out there?" I asked. His dad was the other owner, so in addition to helping with the bodies like I did, Ryan also worked in the chapel and the office. Presumably he'd take over the business someday, since Mr. Ludwig's kids had decided to work among the living.

He shook his head. "My dad and Mr. Ludwig are doing this one."

"Then why are you here?"

"Didn't have any other plans," Ryan said with a shrug. "I thought maybe they could use a hand behind the scenes. Or you could, you know, on cleanup."

Deliberately, he bent, opening a cardboard box and stacking glove packets on a shelf. It wasn't the first time Ryan had showed up for no reason during my shift. He was friendly but never chatty, and I couldn't figure out if he liked me or didn't trust me.

"I'm sure I'll be fine, but thanks." For *nothing.* I bit back frustration. He couldn't know that he was interrupting my research.

I went back to restocking gowns, tissues, tubing, needles—the supplies of managing death.

I spent most Saturdays at Ludwig & Wilton. For my actual job, cleanup, I didn't need to be there until the wake was over. But it only took one Saturday to realize I wouldn't see any mourners that way. So I'd told Mr. Ludwig that Petra had weekend book club meetings at the apartment, making it impossible to study. Did he mind if I came early, maybe helped with the phone or restocking or setup, then studied in the break room before my shift? Of course he didn't.

My school books usually sat on the faux-wood table by the fridge, unopened. Unless Ryan was on.

"I guess I'll go in the back to study," I told him after emptying the last box of eye caps.

Ryan nodded, continuing to work with just a glance up at me.

On my way to the break room, I saw mourners being escorted to the chapel by Mr. Wilton, Ryan's dad. There were four different ways to access the chapel, the large room where wakes were held. It was something Mr. Ludwig was especially proud of. He'd overseen the conversion of this turn-of-the-century mansion to a state-of-the-art funeral home and had soundproof walls, soft-close doors, propping mechanisms, and multiple access points built in to eliminate distraction, his pet peeve. He'd shown me everything on my first-day tour.

"It's like being a magician," Ryan said when Mr. Ludwig stepped away to take a call. He'd been working in the office, its door open to the front hall. "No one wants to see the mechanics behind the tricks."

The break room, however, does not open to the chapel. It's stuffy and windowless with a beat-up table, six plastic chairs, and magazines like *Undertaking Today* and *Next Steps, The Funeral Journey.* I forced myself to sit there for fifteen minutes, looking at my school books without absorbing a thing, fidgety to get back to the action. When I was sure Ryan wasn't coming to check on me, I peeked out the opposite-side door. The back hallway was empty.

I crossed quickly and slipped into the prep room, cringing. You never knew what you'd find there. It's where all the gruesome work was done, and bodies stayed on the steel table for at least a day after embalming to be sure everything went right. Wouldn't want to dress them and *then* find out something leaked. Thankfully, there was no one—dead or alive—in the prep room now and any bodies picked up today wouldn't be brought in until we were ready to embalm. There was a refrigerated area downstairs where they could chill out. Mr. Ludwig's joke, not mine.

My sneakers *squee-squeed* across the waxed linoleum to the hallway that connected the prep room and chapel, the path bodies took for their final farewell. I walked it quickly, stopping by the door, which was propped slightly open by a clip at the top. Another of Mr. Ludwig's illusions, preventing it from "clicking" closed if he needed to come in or out.

I leaned in close, hoping he was nowhere around. He'd freak if he found me eavesdropping like this.

". . . right in the middle of a luncheon. They called an ambulance, but I guess it was too late."

"How awful," a woman murmured.

Not family members. They don't discuss details at the wake. I stifled a sigh, knowing "he's in a better place now" or "at least he didn't suffer" would come next. I kept hoping for something meaningful, but had started to wonder if wake talk ever progressed beyond platitudes. They were part of the ritual, I supposed, like washing the body or saying prayers or old ladies wearing veils, things that happened at just about every viewing we'd done at Ludwig & Wilton, all of them so similar.

I'd thought working here could help me piece together some cohesive understanding of what people believe about death, but it turned out almost all our clients were Catholic and Christian. Hindus cremate, Jews bury the body first, visit afterward, and so on. Those who don't embalm rarely come to places like Ludwig & Wilton, so I only saw one small slice of belief and practice.

Thankfully, Mr. Ludwig knew a ton about religion and mortuary history and liked to talk while he worked. Over body Number Two, he told me that families used to prep the deceased and hold the wake at home. They'd open a window so the soul could leave the room, then close it after two hours in case the soul changed its mind. Clocks would be stopped, mirrors covered, but the rituals of washing and dressing the body done today aren't much different than a century ago. Except instead of laying out your dead grandma on the dining room table, it's done here, at the mortuary.

Religion came up first over Number Three, Mary Margaret Hanley, Catholic, a rosary wrapped around her folded hands. Mr. Ludwig was wrestling with her dress collar and the two-sided tape, but my eyes kept wandering back to those beads wound through her stiff fingers.

"How bad do you have to be to go to hell?" I'd asked him.

"You have to commit a mortal sin," he said.

"Like . . . ?"

Mr. Ludwig waved blindly for the scissors, answering as I

handed them over. "Killing someone. Or stealing. Or committing adultery."

I frowned. "Stealing and murder are hardly the same. You really go to hell for stealing? Forever?"

"Well." Mr. Ludwig glanced up at me. "The *outcome* may be different, but not necessarily the *intent*. Catholics believe a sin is something done deliberately and with full understanding that it's wrong. That could apply equally to each crime."

"But everyone's stolen *something*," I said. "Snuck into a movie, done dine-and-dash, taken candy on a dare. The Catholics can't really believe *all* those people are going to hell. Who would ever get to heaven?"

"Everyone who goes to confession," he said. "That absolves them of sin."

"Even the really bad ones? Like killing someone?"

He smiled at my disbelief. "As long as they are sincere in their repentance, yes."

"That's like the mother of all Get Out of Jail Free cards!" I was amazed. "Why would anyone *not* sin?"

Mr. Ludwig stopped working, resting his hands just short of Mary Margaret on the table, and looked at me. "Would you kill someone if you could get away with it?"

"No."

"Steal?"

"I don't know. Maybe?" I thought about the time Tasha and I were in eighth grade and each stole a pair of socks from the mall. Mine were argyle—black, green, and white. Really cute. I'd never worn them. I don't think Tasha had either. "No," I said. "I don't think I would, actually. I'd feel too guilty."

"Exactly. If you *had* ever stolen"—he raised an eyebrow like he knew what I'd been thinking—"you'd probably still feel bad about it. That's repentance. You can't fake it. You actually have to feel it in your heart, and Catholics believe God knows the difference."

That conversation rolled around in my head the rest of the day, collecting mass like a downhill snowball. People who died with an unconfessed mortal sin were damned to hell, Mr. Ludwig said. If that were true, and I knew they were going to die, I *had* to tell them, regardless of whether they ended up living or not. I couldn't let them burn for eternity just because they hadn't gotten to say they were sorry. I rushed home, madly searching online, elated that the answer was so simple all this time.

It wasn't.

Of course.

Confession and mortal sins and hell were what the *Catholics* believed. The Muslims, on the other hand, thought the Catholics were going to hell because they weren't Muslim. And the Buddhists didn't believe in hell at all.

Back to square one.

But it was the start of our own ritual—Mr. Ludwig's and mine—discussions about religious beliefs interspersed with draining fluids or wiring a jaw so it wouldn't hang open like a broken mailbox.

"Carmen, Betty, thank you so much for coming," I heard from the other side of the chapel door. A family member. I perked up, leaning closer, my hand against the wall for balance.

"Oh, Joshua, I'm so sorry about your father. We'd just seen him at the symposium. He looked so healthy . . . happy . . ."

"I know," Joshua answered. I could picture him, dark and stocky like his father had been, nodding sadly. "It was very sudden."

"How's your mom?"

"A little better. Managing."

I heard a sympathetic sigh, the cluck of a tongue. "He'd told me about the project he'd just started. His research sounded so promising . . ."

What research? If I leaned much closer I'd fall through the door, but I was on high alert. *This* is what I needed to know. Robert Killiam had been a doctor. Might he have done something valuable if he'd lived? Critical? I couldn't change anything for him. But maybe I could for the next one.

"You know you're dead meat if my father or Mr. Ludwig finds you here."

I almost screamed I was so startled by Ryan's whisper, soft against my ear, but he'd anticipated that, slipping a hand gently over my mouth. He was close behind me, his chest against my back, and I could feel his warmth, smell fresh soap on his skin.

"I'm going to let go of you," he whispered, "and we're going to walk to the prep room. Be quiet."

I nodded and he released me. My heart was thudding with the fear of having been caught and, strangely, something else. I hadn't been so close to anyone, touched like that, since Jack. Ryan looked nothing like him, but the way his arms felt wrapped around me was too much of a reminder. It hurt.

Ryan took my hand, his grip firm and gentle at the same time. He studied my eyes for a second as we stood less than a foot apart, then he turned and led me silently down the hall. Neither of us spoke until the prep room door closed behind us.

"What's up with you?" Ryan leaned against the steel table in the center of the room, facing me, his arms crossed. I stood by the door, absently rubbing my hand, still warm from being in his.

I'd been trying to think of an explanation, but the hall is only about twenty feet long—way too short to come up with something good. I shrugged, moved to a nearby counter. It occurred to me that Ryan would probably tell his dad and I'd probably get fired. That would suck because, aside from hoping to learn something, I actually liked working there.

"Really, Cassie," he said. "I've been watching you and something's off. It's like you've got some kind of . . . I don't know . . . sick fascination with death."

"No, it's not that."

"It's not? What is it, then?"

"It's . . . I'm . . ." I wasn't sure how to answer, but fired or not, I didn't want him to think I was a freak. "I'm just trying to learn about it," I said.

Ryan looked skeptical. "What do you mean? Learn what?"

I bit my lip, trying to phrase the truth carefully. "People believe such different things about death, you know? Where do we go? How does it affect the people left behind? What if . . ." I paused, making sure it sounded okay. "What if someone didn't die when they did? Like that guy out there, Dr. Killiam. How would things have been different for his family or, I don't know, the world even, if he were still alive?"

I held my breath, waiting for Ryan's reaction. He just stared, making my ears and face warm. Maybe they *are* bedroom eyes, I thought.

"That's pretty deep," he said finally.

I shrugged. "I'm not perverse or anything. Really. And I promise I won't do it again if you . . ."

Ryan held up his hand. "I'm not going to tell my dad. But seriously, Cassie, you can't do that . . . spy on the wake. You would have scared the crap out of my dad or Mr. Ludwig if they came through there. What if they yelled? How do you think the family would have felt?"

"Yeah, I know."

Ryan walked closer, stopping by the counter perpendicular to mine. He wasn't tall but he looked strong, his body lean, like a mountain biker or rock climber, with solid, tanned arms, even in winter. "So what have you learned so far?"

"Excuse me?" I was still thinking about his arms.

"In your studies here," Ryan said, his gaze direct and amused. "What have you learned?"

"Well . . ." I thought for a few seconds. "I've learned that the body is just a body." I met his eyes, feeling like I needed to prove something. "A vessel. People look different when they're dead. No matter how well Mr. Ludwig sets the features or Victoria does the makeup, it's never quite right because the thing that animates them is missing," I said. "The soul or essence or whatever."

Ryan raised his eyebrows, looking at me speculatively. "Maybe . . . but you know Mr. Ludwig and Victoria work from the outside, not in."

"What do you mean?"

"Think about the stuff we do: using cotton to make the ear-lobes hang right and the cheeks look round, molding the lips to the right fullness and width," Ryan said. "We can use pictures and the body's clues—like where the lips change texture and color—to set the features, but we can't replicate the body's quirks. When people are alive, their brain directs muscles to work a certain way and produce a certain look."

"Huh." That had never occurred to me. I spoke slowly, considering it. "So you think the difference in how they look is totally anatomical and not about the soul leaving the body?"

"It's possible. They might look different for very basic, scientific reasons," Ryan answered, deftly hoisting himself up to sit on the counter. "Have you learned anything else?"

I was still leaning and probably too short to do what Ryan

had done with any grace, so I stayed put. "I've learned that very few people are ready for death. Except maybe the very old or sick," I added, thinking of the man on the bench in Chicago.

Ryan nodded.

"What I've been thinking about a lot lately is the people left behind," I told him. "I mean, what we do here is really about them, right?"

"Of course. Undertaking is for the living," Ryan answered. "We help them say good-bye."

Something about the way he said it made me look at him more carefully, feeling like we'd moved beyond intellectual sparring to a place more personal. "Have you ever lost anyone close to you?" I asked softly. The question was both too forward and anticipated. I could read the answer on his face even before I asked it.

Ryan nodded. "My mom." He said it without averting his eyes or trying to hide the shadow that passed over them. "She died when I was eleven. Cancer. It was the hardest thing I've ever had to deal with."

I nodded.

"I know you've been through it, too," he said. "I'm sure you understand."

"I do." We were silent for a moment and I thought, this isn't how I'd pegged Ryan at all. Maybe I should have. I don't think you can be in this business without a great deal of sensitivity. "I wonder about them," I said finally. "My parents, my grandmother." Mr. McKenzie who got hit by a car, the girl who jumped in New York, Walter Ness. All the people whose deaths I'd had a hand in. "What do you think happens to people when they die?"

Ryan hesitated and I waited for another complex answer, but a voice in the hall surprised us both. Mr. Ludwig. I held my breath, sure he'd come in, but he passed by, probably for supplies that

Ryan or I should have been refilling. When I looked back at Ryan I saw him exhale, then look at his watch. "Jury's still out," he said, pushing off the counter. He landed gracefully on the floor, and I imagined that whatever sport Ryan was into, he was probably very good at it. "We should go," he said. "This"—he gestured toward the chapel, then back to where we stood—"is between us. Not to worry. But be careful."

Then he left, the door shushing closed behind him.

I stayed in the prep room a few more minutes, collecting myself and wondering why I'd never really noticed Ryan before. Of course, I knew he was around, spoke to him almost every shift, but I'd never really *noticed* him.

I wondered what he thought of me.

One thing was certain: Ryan was right, it wasn't smart to snoop around at the wakes. I'd have to find another, less risky way, though I felt like for once I was close to hearing something useful. I was frustrated that I missed the end of what that woman Betty or Carmen had been talking about. Robert Killiam's research. I'd never know what it was; I'd already searched high and low on the Internet. There was nothing there.

I went back to the break room, trying to study for real this time, but I was preoccupied with things that chemistry and calc couldn't begin to eclipse. Ryan. The stuff we'd talked about. The way he'd felt so close to me.

I couldn't put my finger on exactly why, but it had pierced the layers of busyness I'd tried to wrap myself in, bringing back memories of Jack and all the things I was trying to forget. Or at least ignore, for now. Like the day he found me by my locker soon after I'd come home from Kansas.

"Walk you home?"

He'd startled me and I jumped a little, my heart racing as it registered that it was him. Jack. I turned, holding tightly to the books I'd pulled from my locker, and found him watching me, his head tipped slightly to the side, smiling.

"Sure." I leaned back into my locker. "Let me just get my stuff together."

We left school, walking side by side down the wide cement steps. It was my third day back in Ashville and I was still feeling like my old life had broken in half and been haphazardly glued back together. Even things that shouldn't have changed *had*—my walk to school, my friendship with Tasha, the places I liked to go. They were all colored by what had happened and what I'd learned that summer.

I felt especially awkward with Jack because I'd been thinking about him too much. For months. I'd replayed the day I ran into him in Kansas so often—the way he called to me in the park, looked at me, told me he'd broken up with his girlfriend—holding on to it like some kind of desperate touchstone so that now, back in Pennsylvania, I worried that I'd blown it all out of proportion, read things into it that weren't there.

"Tell me about your summer in Kansas," he said, smiling down at me as we started toward my apartment. "Did you like it out there?"

"Not at first," I said, still unsteady, unnatural, though I'd walked beside him, seen his smile and those brown eyes a hundred times. "My aunt just kind of dumped me off at her apartment. I didn't know anyone . . ." I paused, thinking about how bored I'd been. "I moped around for a while, kind of hating it. Then I decided to get a job."

"Oh yeah? Where'd you work?"

I told him about the coffee shop and the people there, feeling more and more like myself, talking to the Jack I'd always known as we walked. He asked me about the town and we swapped stories about how the Midwest was different, pausing only when we reached my apartment.

I hesitated, thinking about asking him in, but knowing that even I didn't want to be there, in that half-packed apartment.

"Do you have to go?" he asked.

"No." I smiled, relieved. "Definitely not."

He smiled back and we continued down the block in a comfortable silence, leaving my building behind.

"Soooo," he finally drawled, teasing. "Is that where you met your boyfriend? At work?"

Immediately any ease I'd felt evaporated. I sensed Jack looking at me but couldn't meet his eyes.

"No," I said, watching my feet scuff along the sidewalk. "We met in a class I took at Lennox U."

I flushed at the idea that Jack knew about Lucas. He couldn't know what had happened between us, but *I* did and somehow, being here with Jack now made all of that seem so wrong.

"Ooh, a *college* guy." Jack was still teasing, but it sounded a little forced. "I thought he looked older."

I didn't answer, wishing I could say it was nothing, but that would be a lie. And I didn't want to lie to Jack. "We broke up," I said finally. "Before I left."

"I'm sorry."

"Thanks," I told him, finally looking up. "But I'm not."

He held my gaze for an extra beat and I could feel something pass between us. Jack smiled a little but didn't answer.

We were in the preserve by then; leafy trees, still fully green, shading the path. I thought he might ask more about Lucas or the class, but he didn't and I was glad. Instead, Jack told me about his visits to the Midwest, the schools that he'd seen, until he stopped near a clearing, watching me with an expectant smile.

"Do you know where you are?"

The leaves of the Japanese maple towering over us were just starting to turn purple at their edges. In another month they'd be bright orange, and when you were up in the tree, the sun filtering through them as it sank low in the sky made it feel like you were inside the sunset. "Of course," I told him, shielding my eyes to search the branches.

"It's gone," he said.

I looked at him, eyes wide, surprised how sharp my disappointment was.

Jack smiled gently. "I felt the same way. Even climbed up to be sure."

I squinted back up into the tree like he might be wrong and the old wooden platform that we'd used as a fort would be there, waiting for us. It had been ancient when we'd found it, leftover from when the preserve had been private land. We were nine that summer.

I looked back at him and shrugged as if it didn't matter. "Bummer."

"Yeah," he agreed, circling to the other side of the tree.

"I wonder how long it's been gone," I said. "I don't think I've been back here since I was ten or eleven." The summer after Jack had moved across town.

"You came without me?" Jack raised his eyebrows in mock disapproval.

"Not much," I said honestly, thinking how dull it had been sitting up there without Jack to play chess or pirates or I Spy with. "It wasn't the same."

He nodded, swinging our bookbags to the ground and sitting on the big flat rock a few feet away. I walked over to join him.

We were quiet for a minute, then he said, "That's how I felt this summer, you know."

I looked at him and he flashed me a small smile before looking back at our tree.

"What do you mean?"

"It wasn't the same with you gone," Jack said.

My breath caught. I wanted so much to believe it, but Jack and I hadn't been close since the summer we found the fort. Eight years ago. I told him that.

"I know. But . . ." He looked over at me, serious and a little uncertain. "I've always felt . . . I don't know, still . . . connected?" He gave a small, embarrassed laugh. "That probably doesn't make any sense."

"No," I said quietly. "It does."

He scratched at the rock as he spoke, his voice soft but steady. "At first I didn't even realize you'd left. It sounds terrible. I mean, what kind of friend am I or how much connection can there be if I don't even know you're gone, right?" He glanced up and I shrugged, thinking that's exactly what I'd expected. That he wouldn't even notice. "But one day I realized that I kept looking for you," Jack continued. "In the stands at games, at parties, at the pool. I don't think I knew it before, but it was something I'd always done. Just kind of . . . keeping tabs on you. Making sure you were around." He glanced down at his hands, absently rubbing at a finger, then back up at me. "I always felt better when you were."

It was my turn to look down, a little overwhelmed by Jack's description of things I'd always felt and done myself, never imagining he might be doing them too.

"When it hit me that you just . . . weren't here, I couldn't believe

it. Even after Tasha told me what happened. I went by your apartment, eventually found myself here."

"You did?"

He nodded. "I'm not even sure how to describe how I felt . . . sad
is the closest, I guess. Like things weren't quite right. Like . . ." He
hesitated, searching my face, holding my eyes as he said, "Like I
missed out on something important."

I couldn't speak, feeling such a rush of hope and happiness
and fear all together.

"And then I saw you in Kansas. I mean, what are the chances of
that happening? And you were with a guy. Your boyfriend. And
I . . ." Jack took a deep breath. "I tried to be cool and everything,
but I realized that all this time I've kept track of you not just
because we were friends, but because deep down, I thought someday we'd be more. I realized I *wanted* us to be more. And it hit me
that you might go away. Like you did." He was watching me. "Or
find someone else. Like you did. It hit me that I might have
already missed my chance."

"You didn't." I said it so quietly he might not have heard,
except for the silence of the preserve, the wind still as if to be sure
neither of us would miss out this time.

Jack didn't say anything and what we'd just admitted hung
between us, delicate and scary. Then he reached over, his hand
warm, grazing my cheek, lifting my chin. He leaned close, my
heart thudding as he whispered in my ear, "Then let's make sure"—
his lips brushed my skin—"we don't." I felt the slight scratchiness
of his cheek as he drew back, his lips just barely apart from mine.
We hesitated, savoring the seconds that had taken us so long to get
to. The closeness of him was almost unbearable. I couldn't think,
speak, breathe. I could only want.

And then we kissed. Soft and sweet and hot and tender and as brilliant as the flame-colored leaves we used to play in. Like it was meant to be: fated, destined.

Only maybe it wasn't. Because I was here, seven hundred miles away, in the break room of a funeral home. And Jack was still where I'd left him.

Mr. Ludwig called me to the chapel finally, after the family and mourners had gone. Mechanically, I folded the chairs and tables, hoping work could push away the memories and let me refocus on what I'd seen and heard in the chapel today. The reason I was here and not with Jack.

I forced myself to stand by the now-closed coffin of James Killiam and think of how he'd looked the last time I saw him, whatever part of him still remained. Caked in makeup, wearing a suit he probably hated while alive—clothed in now for eternity. Or at least until bugs ate it away.

If I had seen him with the mark, would I have told? Given him a chance to save himself? Of course. He was a good man and citizen. He had a family who loved him. He was a doctor and probably saved lives. And there was that tantalizing research.

He shouldn't have died.

For every soul extended days, another is cut short.

Except the letter made the whole equation different.

I texted Jack on the bus ride home, yearning for that day in the preserve, wishing I could go back and live in it forever, far from the mark and its uncertain responsibilities.

"made a new friend at work today. how r u?"

As usual, there was no response.

chapter 6

Liv was waiting for me outside calc. She had Algebra II that same period, right next door.

"How'd it go?" she asked.

"Meh." I'd studied a little the night before, until Petra convinced me to play Scrabble. I was pretty sure I'd passed the test, but probably not by much. "Not great."

"I don't know why you signed up for calc, Cassie."

"Masochism?"

"Must be." Liv and I began walking down the hall. Usually, she'd start in right away on the crazy-cool outfit Mrs. Steingartner was wearing or what they were working on in art, or at least what she'd done the night before, but today Liv was quiet. And frowning.

"Everything okay?" I asked.

"Huh?" She glanced over, still lost in thought. "Yeah." Liv scratched her ear, pushed up her glasses, then asked not quite off-handedly, "Hey, you think the restaurant you work at is hiring?"

"Uh . . . I'm not sure," I said carefully. The little white lie had been a lot easier than explaining why I worked where I really did. "Why?"

"I was just thinking maybe I should get a job."

"Really?" In Ashville, all my friends had jobs. Here, none of them did. These kids didn't need to work and their parents didn't want them to. Especially Liv's.

"Yeah." She shrugged, but didn't look at me, confirming something was definitely up and she didn't want to talk about it. "You think you could find out?"

She glanced over quickly, just long enough for me to see the worry line between her brows.

"Sure." What else could I say? But I was already cringing at my next set of lies—*sorry, they're not hiring*—and how disappointed she'd be. Maybe I could pick up some applications for her beforehand.

We crossed the hallway and I glanced to the left. Zander's locker was down there, but he wasn't.

Liv changed the subject. "You doing anything Saturday?" she asked. "Erin and I were talking about going to the movies, if you want to come."

"That'd be great. I have to work but should be done by six or so."

"And then you'll need to run home and shower," Liv said, taking the stairs two at a time like Jack used to. "You don't want to smell like a french fry."

Or a dead person. Which reminded me I'd meant to ask about Ryan. I kept my voice super casual, knowing how Liv pounced on stuff like this. "Hey, do you know anyone at Southridge?"

"Yup. A girl who used to live on my block goes there. Why?"

"Nothing really. Just this guy I met . . ."

"Ooohhh!" Liv's face lit up and she grabbed my arm, her eyes sparkling. I knew she'd been waiting for this since I told her about Jack and I was glad to see her frown disappear, but I wasn't into Ryan like that.

She'd dragged the story out of me—what little I'd tell—one day at her house. It wasn't long after she'd invited me to their lunch table and we were hanging out, just the two of us.

"Yeah," I answered. "I had a boyfriend. We broke up before I left. His name was Jack." Even saying it stung. I'd thought that would stop. Not right away, of course. But it was as bad then as now and each of the eighty-four days in between.

I gave Liv only sketchy details, but she totally saw through my no-big-deal-we-broke-up spiel. I could see her rooting for me any-time I showed any interest in a guy. Like now.

"Spill it!" Liv said, grinning like a madman. "Who is he?"

"It's not like that," I told her, already regretting the conversa-tion. "I met him at work and was just curious . . ."

"Name, Cassie. I need a name."

"Ryan Wilton."

She shook her head. "Nope, never heard of him."

I waved my hand dismissively. "Yeah, that's okay . . ." The sooner this ended, the better. I'd just been hoping to get a better handle on Ryan. What he was like outside the funeral parlor. I'd tried looking him up online, but he wasn't on any of the social sites. Then again, neither was I.

"I can ask my friend."

"No. Really, Liv, you don't need to. I was just curious, but for real, it's no biggie."

"Is he cute?"

I shrugged. "Not bad. But I'm not into him or anything."

"Uh-huh." Liv grinned, rubbing her hands together eagerly. "I'll let you know what I find out."

Ugh.

I took the El to the city again, my nerves jangling as I sped closer to Demetria, wondering if today would be the day. I tried to tell myself the whole thing was probably a wild-goose chase, but something wouldn't let me let go of the idea that what I needed was locked inside her.

She was on the itchy tweed couch, in the same spot as the last time. In the same shapeless gown too. I looked around, feeling like I'd stepped into a time warp, but the nurse at the door was different, so were the other patients. Medicine Man was, thankfully, nowhere to be seen.

"Hi, Demetria," I said, quietly settling into the chair next to her. "It's me again. Cassie."

Her eyes stayed fixed somewhere beyond me. I sighed, trying not to show my disappointment. Across the room, an old woman sat rocking and staring out the window. Two guys faced each other across a checkerboard with no checkers. If you weren't crazy already, spending a few days here would probably do the trick.

I turned back to her. "You know how last time I was talking about the Greeks at my school? How I'd hoped to meet some when I came here?" Rhetorical questions, though I hadn't necessarily meant them to be. "There's this thing . . ." I paused, backtracking, not completely ready to be so direct with this girl I didn't know at all. "Well, a strange thing happened to me a few weeks ago. There was this man—an old guy, just sitting out in the freezing cold. I saw something on him. The mark . . ."

My words—already hushed—trailed off into the quiet of the

room. I was at a loss for how to say enough without saying too much. I looked down at my hands, fingers woven tightly together, and took a deep breath, almost started talking again.

But when I glanced back up, Demetria was staring at me.

I inhaled sharply because it wasn't just that her eyes met mine. There was comprehension in them. I could tell she was listening, had heard every word I'd said. Understood them, maybe on a deeper level.

"Demetria?" It was barely more than a whisper.

She didn't speak, but kept staring, an unearthly, penetrating look.

This time I did whisper. "Do you know what that means? The mark?"

Her eyes slowly drifted away from mine, back toward the wall. Her hands lay in her lap, wrists still bandaged.

"Demetria?"

Nothing.

"Demetria?" Her eyes were unfocused, attention clouding over. I was losing her. "C'mon, Demetria, listen to me!"

I was louder than I'd meant to be. The nurse stood up. "Is there a problem, Miss"—she glanced down at her visitors' log—"Renfield?"

Damn! "No. I'm sorry." Now she'd remember me. And not in a good way. "She just . . . I thought she was . . ."

"You can't talk to the patients like that." She took a step closer, her face stern, reminding me of what I'd promised Petra.

"No, I know. I'm sorry," I said again, feeling truly ashamed. What was I thinking? I was going to scare Demetria and get myself banned from visiting.

"Keep your voice down or you'll have to leave." She went back to her table, shooting me one more dirty look. She scribbled something and I hoped it was only an answer to the crossword puzzle she'd been working on.

Demetria seemed not to have noticed, back to staring at the wall.

I leaned closer. "I think you can hear me, Demetria." I kept my voice low and soft, trying to coax her out. "And if you understand me, if you know what I'm talking about, I can kind of see why you . . ." I glanced at her wrapped wrists. "Why you're here. It can drive you . . ." No, don't say crazy. "Um, well, it can make things hard. Really hard."

She didn't look at me, but she blinked. A sign?

"I need your help," I told her. "If you know anything about it . . . please . . . I'm kind of on my own here."

She didn't move and her eyes were still far away. In my heart I knew we were done. I glanced back at the nurse, wondering if it'd be okay to touch Demetria, just to get her attention, try one more time to make some kind of connection. That's when I saw him. Zander Dasios. Standing by the window. I was sure of it this time.

Immediately, he stepped out of view.

I looked at Demetria—still out to lunch—then walked quickly to the doorway.

"All done?" the nurse asked.

I shook my head. "Just need the ladies' room."

I opened the door, my heart pounding at the thought of talking to Zander, but the hallway was empty.

I looked left and right, trotted to one end, then the other. Deserted. I stopped at the nurses' station.

"There was a guy here a minute ago. I saw him looking through the window in the lounge. Did he come back this way?"

The lady at the desk looked up from a stack of paperwork. "Didn't notice."

"He didn't check out?"

"No. But a lot of visitors don't."

"Well, can you tell me when he checked in?"

She frowned, but seeming eager to be rid of me, pulled out the log sheet, running her finger down it.

"The last visitor, before you, checked in at 3:06 p.m."

But it wasn't him. The name next to her finger was Joe Liguori. Zander's name was nowhere on the list.

She saw me looking and closed the book. "Visitor information is confidential."

"I'm sorry," I said. "Does everyone who comes up here have to sign in?"

"Everyone," she answered emphatically. I believed her. I'd never gotten more than two steps onto the floor before someone was asking if they could help me.

I walked slowly back to the lounge, thinking how the brain works in funny ways, taking the unlikely scenario of Zander being here and turning it into the ridiculous. Because the first thing I'd thought—my insides doing a fluttery spin at the idea—was that Zander was here because he'd followed me.

I was embarrassed it even crossed my mind. I mean, really. He'd decided the mental hospital was the perfect place to ask me out? Even though he'd never talked to me at school? Right. I shook my head.

Demetria was being escorted out of the lounge when I returned.

"Visiting time is over," the nurse said.

"But I just ran to the bathroom."

"Bathroom's at the other end of the hall."

"Oh. Yeah, well, I got lost."

She shook her head. "It's time for her meds. You'll have to come back another day."

"Okay," I said, forcing myself not to argue. "Bye, Demetria. I'll be back soon."

Out of habit, I texted Jack on the train ride home: "visited a friend at the hospital today. she's greek—getting in touch with my roots."

And I felt like I was. Inching closer to the answers. It hadn't been much, but the way she'd looked at me . . . I felt sure I'd connected with Demetria.

They say three's a charm. Maybe my next visit would be the one.

chapter 7

I asked Petra about my Zander sighting when I got home that night. It was after eight and she was just starting on a pizza. "Grab a slice," she said. She didn't need to offer twice.

"Nope," Petra said flatly, between bites. "No way someone could have gotten on the floor without signing in. Not with the desk right by the entry. They're too strict."

"That's what I thought. But what if he used a fake name?"

She shrugged. "He could have, but he'd need ID to go with it."

"Yeah, but it's not like it would have to be anything all that official. I mean, he wasn't trying to buy beer, just visit crazy people."

"True. But why, Cassie? Why would he bother?"

She had me there. Was I really still clinging to the idea that he'd followed me? I shook my head. It had been Joe Liguori and not Zander after all, though it *had* looked so much like him.

"Unless he's the father of her baby," Petra said casually.

"What?"

"I saw it when I was checking her file today," Petra said,

leaning forward, her eyes gleaming. Sometimes I thought she'd become a psychiatrist just because she was nosy, the smartest person I knew who still read the *National Enquirer* and *US Weekly*. "It's part of the standard blood work; the results came back a few days ago."

"Wow." I let the idea—pregnant—roll around for a few seconds, like a marble toward the chute of a funnel. Being a single teen mother would be bad. The responsibility of the mark was awful. What if the two were combined—Demetria realizing she was about to pass her visions on to someone else?

Petra was nodding, still leaning forward, elbows on her knees. "Demetria hasn't said anything about it to her therapist. Of course, she still hasn't said anything *at all* to her therapist."

"Are you sure she knows? About being pregnant?"

"The hCG levels in her blood put her at about eleven weeks. That's two missed periods. It's possible she hasn't realized it, but I'm guessing she has. It might even explain . . ."

". . . why she's there," I finished for Petra.

"Exactly."

And then what Petra said before came back to me. The part about Zander. She'd been joking, but what if she was right? A player, Liv had called him, as if I'd needed her to tell me that. As if it weren't totally apparent looking at him. Was he the father? That would be a reason to hide his identity. I was disappointed to think he might be exactly what he seemed.

"What about her parents?" I asked, ignoring thoughts of Zander. "Do they know?"

Petra held out the box with the last slice of pizza, pulling it onto her plate when I declined. "I don't think so. I imagine they'd have mentioned it at admission. I think Demetria's the only one who knows."

"Demetria and maybe the boy," I corrected.

"Right," Petra agreed. "And maybe the boy."

Saturday at the funeral home was a bummer: a wake where almost no one came, the worst kind. The guy wasn't old, maybe fifty. He'd died of lung cancer.

I'd been disappointed, too, that Ryan wasn't around. I'd thought about our conversation a lot, sure he thought I was some kind of weirdo.

But when I went to my locker at the end of the shift, a stack of books was waiting: *Death, Dying, and Religion*; *Coming to Grips with Death*; and *The Ultimate Journey*.

There was also a note:

Thought these would feed your non-perverse fascination.

Enjoy.
Ryan

It made me smile.

"How's *My Guy* sound?" Liv asked as I slid into her car, idling outside my apartment building just after seven.

I grimaced. "Horrible."

She laughed. "Yeah, I told Hannah no chick flicks. *Zombie Queen II?*"

"Much better."

We were meeting Erin, Hannah, and her friend Pete at the mall. I wasn't a huge fan of the mall. Shopping was fine, but there were always a lot of people there and lots of people meant more risk of seeing the mark.

"So my friend knew that guy you asked about," Liv said, pulling sharply in front of a car on our left so she'd make the light. Liv was a frightening driver. If I ever saw the mark on her, I'd demand she hand over her keys.

"Oh yeah?" I said casually. I had to hide a grin, thinking of his note on the books. I didn't want Liv to read anything into it.

"Yeah."

I waited. Nothing. "Well?"

"Oh!" Liv feigned surprise, looking over at me wide eyed. "You want to hear about him?"

"Ha-ha."

"My bad," she said, smiling and weaving through traffic way too fast. "I thought you weren't into him or anything."

"I'm not," I answered, gripping the seat. "But since your friend went to the trouble and all, you might as well tell me."

"Riiight. Well, for starters, his family owns a funeral parlor." Liv paused dramatically. "And he works there."

"Uh-huh."

"You knew that." She sounded disappointed.

"Yeah, I did."

"But I thought you said you worked with him."

I had, hadn't I? "Uh . . ." I could see that playing out the lie about my job was about to get trickier than just telling her they weren't hiring. I liked Liv and decided to come clean instead, hoping she'd understand. "I *do* work with him."

She glanced over, frowning. "So . . . he works at a restaurant too?"

"No." I paused for a second, wondering if this was really a good idea. "Actually, I don't work at a restaurant."

"You don't?"

I shook my head. "I work at a funeral parlor. The one Ryan's dad owns."

"Huh?" Liv looked over, her nose crinkling as she squinted at me. Totally confused. I wished she'd put her eyes back on the road.

"I didn't tell you guys because I thought you'd think it was gross."

"It *is* gross."

"Yeah, it is kinda," I admitted. "But it's good money and it's actually sort of interesting."

"Um . . . once you get past the dead bodies and stuff?"

"Right."

Liv was quiet and I wondered if she was mad, freaked out, or both. Or maybe trying to decide whether to take me home or just drop me by the side of the road. At least it was suburbia. I could definitely get back to the apartment from here.

"Liv?"

"Yeah?" She was still frowning, but her voice wasn't angry.

"I'm sorry I lied. I wasn't sure how you guys—Hannah and Erin especially—would take it. A restaurant sounded like a more normal job."

"It is." Liv flicked her turn signal. Left, toward the mall. I guess she wasn't going to dump me off just yet. "I don't think I'd tell them about your real job."

"No, probably not."

"They'd think it's creepy, for sure."

"But you don't?" I asked hopefully.

"No, it's creepy all right." Liv stopped at the light just before the mall and grinned at me. "But where else would I get to hear about dead bodies and hot guys all in the same place?"

I smiled back, more relieved than I would have guessed. I

wasn't here to make friends, but as I'd learned in Kansas, being in a new place is hard enough. Being there totally on your own is a lot harder. I would have missed Liv.

"I guess this means you can't hook me up with a job, huh?"

"Well, I don't know," I said, trying not to smile. "I could talk to my boss . . ."

"Kidding!" Liv shrieked. "I do *not* want to work there!"

I laughed. "What? Dead bodies, hot guys, what's not to like?" She was laughing too and I decided to ask. "So why the sudden job search anyway?"

Liv's smile vanished immediately. She sighed, hesitating long enough that I thought she might not answer. Then she said, "My dad lost his job."

"Oh no." I kicked myself for bringing it up, but that hadn't occurred to me at all. I'd thought maybe she wanted something her parents wouldn't buy. Although, having seen her room, it was hard to imagine what that might be. "I'm really sorry, Liv."

"Yeah, thanks," she said. "It's not like we're going to be destitute or anything. I just . . . I don't know. I thought maybe I should try to help out."

"I bet that'd mean a lot to your parents," I said, surprised by her thoughtfulness. I probably shouldn't have been. Liv was quirky and fun, but she wasn't shallow. "If you want help applying and stuff, I could make the rounds with you," I said. "I actually already started a list of some places you could try . . ."

"Since your *restaurant* wouldn't have hired me?" she said pointedly.

"Yeah. Exactly."

She smiled. "That'd be cool. I've never done it before, so some help would be great." Liv looked over, biting her lip. "About my dad, though . . . I don't really want everyone to know."

"Don't worry, Liv," I said quickly. "It's totally between us."

"Thanks." Neither of us said anything for a minute, the silence not awkward, but not really comfortable either, the way it is when you find yourself somewhere a little more intense than you meant to be.

"Sooo," I said finally, "want to go back to talking about hot guys?"

"Absolutely!" Liv grinned, tires squealing as she swung into a spot and shut off the car. "Hot guys who work with dead people."

"Okay." I sighed in mock exasperation. "Tell me what your friend said about Ryan." Having Liv tease me about my supposed crush was a lot better than having her think too much about the whole dead-bodies thing. Or about how I'd lied. Or about the problems with her dad.

"She said he's a brainiac—AP classes, Scholar's Bowl, that sort of thing—but he's got an awesome bod." Liv raised an eyebrow, looking devilish. "True?"

I thought of how he'd felt behind me at the chapel door; strong arms, broad shoulders. The way he moved, both athletic and graceful. "Yeah." I nodded, getting out of the car. "He's not bad."

"Well, he's not seeing anyone," she yelled over the roof, slamming her door shut against the wind and motioning me to hurry. "She said he spends a lot of time working, which of course she thought was weird. You know, because of *where* he works." Liv nudged my arm as we jogged toward the mall.

I nodded. "It's not that bad when you get used to it."

"Uh, okay." We'd reached the entrance. Liv paused with her hand on the door handle and turned to me. "So, did he ask you out or what?"

"No! Nothing like that," I said, opening the other door to walk in ahead of her. "I told you I was just curious. I'm not into him or anything." Not really. Though he was interesting. And maybe a little hot.

"Oh." Liv paused, biting her lip. "So I shouldn't have told my friend to let him know you'd asked?"

"What?" I stopped dead, turning to face her. "You didn't."

She laughed out loud. "No. I didn't." Liv started down the mall again. "Let's go, we'll miss the previews."

It was an hour and a half of totally ridiculous brain sucking and shambling. The dead people and brains didn't even look realistic.

Afterward, we stood outside the theater. Erin and Liv were talking to some guy, Nick, from their art class, but Hannah dragged me away, rolling her eyes. "We'll rescue them from Loserville later," she said. Instead I got to listen to her friend Pete talk about his car. At excruciating length. I couldn't have been happier when he glanced over my shoulder, stopping in midsentence to yell "Max!", gave us the barest of "see ya's," and trotted over to a dark-haired girl by the music store.

"He's had a crush on her forever," Hannah said petulantly, staring after him. "Maxine Perkins. She goes to Wexford Academy."

"Oh yeah?" A group of guys and girls came out of the store, sauntering toward where Max and Pete were laughing and talking. I started to ask Hannah if she wanted to grab some ice cream when I saw Zander Dasios at the rear of the group. I felt heat rising to my cheeks immediately.

"Let's go over and talk to them," Hannah said, her mouth set in a tight "I'm going to get my guy back" line.

"Oh, I don't know." I took a step backward, the idea of coming face-to-face with Zander a little overwhelming, but Hannah already had her arm hooked through mine, pulling me relentlessly toward them.

Zander looked up as we approached. Our eyes met and a smirk caught the corner of his lip. I looked away, my mind spinning. I'd never spoken to him, never been closer than across the hall at school, yet somehow I felt he knew things about me. He was that kind of guy, overly aware of the effect he had on girls.

I stood by Hannah's side, a fake smile pasted on my lips, cringing at how she forced herself into the conversation, loud and too happy. I couldn't see Zander but knew he was near, sensed him somewhere behind me.

I turned, casually glancing over my shoulder to find him leaning against the wall, ten feet back, with his head cocked slightly to the side. Watching me.

I looked away, my heart pounding. He wasn't really looking at *me*, I thought. Just at the group—all of us—wondering when his friends would be done, ready to get ice cream or have a cigarette or whatever types like him did. I tried to ignore that he was there and focus on the conversation, but Pete's words were meaningless gibberish, my mind completely occupied with the way it had felt to have Zander's eyes connect with mine.

I knew I shouldn't, that I'd look like a fool, but I couldn't resist. Stupid, stupid, stupid, I thought even as I did it: turned my head to glance back over my shoulder.

Zander was still staring at me. He raised his eyebrows expectantly. Waiting for me.

Hesitantly, I stepped away from the group, their conversation fading to a mumble as I walked toward him, stopping close enough to see the fineness of his dark eyelashes.

"Hi," I said, after a few seconds of silence that stretched uncomfortably, though Zander didn't seem to notice. "I'm Cassie."

He nodded. "I know."

He was still watching me quietly, smiling a little. Making me fidget. I clasped my hands behind my back so they'd stop. "This is the part where you say, 'I'm Zander,'" I told him.

"But you already know who I am."

"Yes," I admitted, "but it's the polite thing to do. It's called small talk."

Slowly he grinned, his eyes never leaving mine, and he shifted from the wall to hold out his hand. "Hi, Cassie. I'm Zander."

I reached out, slipping my hand in his, visualizing zombie brain fests to forget about the way my whole body tingled from touching him.

"Now what?" he asked.

"Huh?"

He withdrew his hand from mine and I felt the gentle friction of his palm on my skin. He folded his arms languidly across his chest, completely relaxed and confident as he leaned against the wall. "What do we do now, oh goddess of social convention?"

"Well . . . we can say 'nice to meet you' and go our separate ways. Or we can talk."

Zander thought for a minute. "Let's talk. You go first."

"Okay." I tried to think of something witty or interesting to say, but I was flustered around him in a way I couldn't remember ever being and what came out was, "I saw you at the hospital."

Zander looked at me speculatively. "You saw me at the hospital." He said it carefully, drawing out the words as if trying to extract meaning.

I felt my face grow warm. Idiot. Not how you start a conversation. Not the very first time you talk to this tantalizing guy who looks at you with a gleam in his eye and purposely drew you away from his friends and yours.

Somehow, standing next to Zander, the idea of him at the hospital, him being the father of Demetria's baby, seemed utterly ridiculous. He could have his pick of girls. Why would he choose a crazy one? What was I thinking?

But the words were already out, so I forced myself to hold his gaze and finish what I'd started. "Right. That's what I said."

"What are you talking about?"

"Downtown," I said. "Vauxhall Hospital. I was visiting a patient and I thought I saw you. At the window."

"You did, huh?" His eyes were locked on mine. Reaching into the deepest parts of me. It made my throat tighten. And then he shifted his gaze away, idly scanning the crowd around us as if there must be something—anything—more interesting out there. "So?" he said.

"So . . ." I tried not to stammer or notice how cold it felt to have lost his attention. "So was it you? What were you doing there?"

He turned back to me. "What were you?"

I stared mutely.

"I could ask you the same thing," he said, his voice teasing but with a sharper edge. "What were *you* doing there? Vauxhall is a mental hospital. You have friends there?"

"No. I mean, not really. Not that there's anything wrong with that." I'd lost my footing, backpedaling stupidly to get Zander on friendly ground, though it felt like I'd already lost the chance.

He shrugged. "No. Probably not a fun place to hang out, though." He turned as one of his friends called to him from across the way. Zander held up his index finger, signaling he'd be right over. "I've gotta go," he said, glancing down at me.

And then he reached out, his hand brushing my shoulder lightly, making me shiver, and plucked at a purple feather stuck in my hair. From that store with trashy handbags and earrings that Hannah'd dragged me into.

Zander freed the feather. I saw it drop lazily to the ground, but his hand still hovered, inches from my face, a few strands of hair caught between the fingers. I stood motionless, my heart pounding. I was afraid to breathe, not even sure I could. Zander twirled my hair lazily, thoughtfully. It felt intimate, like we were lounging on a blanket in a field somewhere instead of standing outside the movie theater at the Willowbrook Mall.

"You have beautiful hair," he said, his voice low, eyes—*definitely* bedroom eyes—studying mine. "I love girls with long hair. Don't ever cut it." He drew his hand back gently, careful not to pull, letting the dark wisps disengage on their own. He held my eyes for an extra second in a way that made my face burn. "See you around, Cassandra."

Zander sauntered off, not looking back, but knowing I was watching him. Which I was. I couldn't help it.

"Cassaahhndrahhh." Liv mimicked Zander's inflection as she came to stand beside me. I wondered how much else she'd heard. "That's sooo sexy. And the way he was touching you—ooo-la-la."

"Please, Liv." I hardly had the heart to argue because she was right. I kept replaying the way he'd looked at me, called me by my full name the way no one else did. I was surprised he even knew it.

"I was worried about you guys," she said with feigned concern. "I thought you might need to get a room." Liv laughed at her own joke while I blushed hot pink.

She shook her finger at me. Teasing, but not really. "You've got it bad for a bad, bad boy, Cassie. Better to stick with your funeral home romance. It might be weird and a little twisted, but it's probably not nearly as dangerous as getting close to Zander Dasios."

He'd said the word "love." I imagined it on his lips, the context different, and knew Liv was right.

But I had a feeling it was too late.

chapter 8

I couldn't sleep. An insomniac combination of zombies and Zander.

I thought about texting Jack but I felt guilty, like I'd cheated on him. Even though we weren't together. Even though I'd done nothing more than stand next to Zander. Let him play with my hair.

The emptiness of Jack's silence would be too hard tonight anyway. It was so unlike him to hold a grudge, I'd been really surprised and hurt at first when he didn't respond to my messages. I kept thinking he might. I've gone over and over how things ended and I guess I couldn't have handled it much worse. But even now I'm not sure what I would change. The essential problem is the same: the mark is the mark is the mark.

It was dusk of a warm day in late October and we were at the preserve again, not near our tree, but on the rocks overlooking Miller's Pond. I'd been trying to keep up the conversation about school and tests, but I couldn't stop thinking about the woman with the mark I'd warned a few weeks before, my second since going back to Ashville.

I saw her on my way to school. She was walking with a friend, dressed in sweats—the clean, pressed, matching kind that looked like they never saw any actual sweat. I should have followed them, skipped school and tailed her back to her house, waited until she was alone. But I had a calc quiz that day, one I'd studied hard for. For once I felt ready, sure of a good grade, one I thought I deserved and might need for college.

So I walked right up to her, tried to speak quietly, pull her away from her friend so we'd have some privacy. But she didn't hear well and her friend refused to take the hint.

She died anyway.

That part was bad, but even worse was her friend. The one who'd listened to everything I'd said. The one who saw me downtown just a few days ago. She'd run after me demanding that I stop. She needed to talk to me.

"... sent, do you?"

It took me a few seconds to realize I was at the preserve. With Jack, who was waiting for an answer. A few seconds too long. "I'm sorry, Jack," I said. "What did you say?"

Jack shook his head and looked away. "It doesn't matter."

"No, it does. I'm sorry. I was just zoning, but I'm with you now. Really." I touched his arm to be sure he knew.

He didn't move and that was a bad sign. He should have smiled or reached over to hold my hand. That's what he'd normally do.

"Jack."

He looked at me and I felt my stomach drop at the things I saw in his eyes: sadness, resignation.

"Listen," I said earnestly, "I'm sorry I've been a little distracted. I've got some stuff on my mind, things to take care of. It's nothing to do with you."

"What kind of stuff? What things to take care of?"

I tried to hold his gaze, but his eyes were too penetrating. Daring me to be brave enough to tell.

Which of course, I wasn't.

I shrugged. "Just . . . stuff." I tried for the obvious. "You know, things with Nan, her will, um . . . schools. It isn't you."

He nodded. "Right. Except that it is, Cassie. Whatever's bothering you is big enough that it's always with you. I can see it, like a cloud in your eyes, something that's keeping you from committing to anything else. Even when you're with me, you aren't really. Not a hundred percent. Whatever it is, I'd like to help." He took my hands then, seeming so small in his, and looked deep into my eyes. "But you won't let me, Cass. You know how I feel about you and I think you feel the same about me. I don't know why you won't tell me and let me help, but you won't and I feel like an outsider. Like I'm always second best to whatever this thing is."

He waited. This was my chance, I knew. My last one.

It made me tear up because I didn't want to lose Jack and I would if I didn't tell him. "You're not second to anything with me, Jack," I said. It was the best I could do, but it wasn't enough. Especially since it wasn't true. I wanted it to be, but the mark *did* cloud everything, and until I figured it out, nothing would be quite right.

We didn't break up then and there, but that was the day I knew we would. The day I put it in motion.

Three weeks later, I told him.

"I'm leaving, Jack." I'd asked him to walk me home, said we needed to talk. I hadn't bothered assuring him it wasn't as ominous as it sounded. We both knew it was.

He nodded, but didn't say anything. We'd had a fight the day before. Something stupid. By then our fights usually were. I could feel us at the thinnest part of a relationship so frayed we were ready to fall through. I think that's what he thought I meant— that I was leaving him, leaving our relationship. Which I was, but also more.

"You're right about there being something else," I told him. "I can't tell you about it now, but I hope someday—when I've got it figured out—I can."

He looked at me, residual anger replaced by something not much better: disappointment. There was little worse than feeling I'd let Jack Petroski down.

"It isn't you," I said, thinking how, if it weren't already a cliché, my overuse of that line these past two months would have made it one. "If it were something I could tell anyone, you'd be the first. It's just . . . it's a family thing that I have to figure out on my own."

"Cassie," he started. "Whatever it is—"

I held up a hand. "I can't."

He nodded.

"I've bought my tickets, talked to guidance and all that . . ."

He stopped short, my real meaning sinking in. "You're leaving Ashville?"

I nodded.

"Where will you go?" He wasn't sure if I was kidding or maybe just floating the idea with no real plans to act.

"Chicago," I said, the firmness of that one word clarifying how serious I was. "I have a friend out there, a girl I met in Kansas over the summer." Or at least she'd be out there soon. We'd been arranging everything over the past two weeks, since I'd told Petra my emancipation paperwork had come through and I was thinking of leaving. I was shocked when she suggested that she come, too. Then elated. The semiregular e-mails we'd exchanged since I'd left Kansas turned into nightly phone calls as we planned the details, both of us ready and needing to leave things behind.

"When?"

This was the part I was really dreading. "Monday." I grimaced, waiting for his anger.

But Jack was only confused. "Monday? You don't mean four days from now Monday, do you?"

I nodded, still grimacing.

He frowned, getting it. "What about your apartment? The emancipation and will and other legal stuff you've been working on with that lawyer?"

"It's all done. Taken care of."

"So you've been planning this all along?" He asked incredulously. The anger I'd been expecting worked its way into his voice. "You knew you were leaving? How long, Cassie? Since you've been back? Didn't give me much of a chance, did you?"

"It's not like that, Jack. I—"

It was his turn to hold up a hand. "That's okay. Spare me the excuses. I get it now. Sorry I was such an idiot before. I thought we . . ." Jack shook his head. "Forget it."

"You thought we what, Jack?"

"Nothing." He adjusted his backpack. "Good luck, Cass."

"Wait. Don't leave yet, Jack."

"Why not? You are."

And that was it. He turned and walked away.

I told myself that someday I'd work up the nerve to tell him about the mark, but it was a hollow thought because, really, why would he wait around to hear it? And even if he did, how could I tell? He might understand, but it would change how he looked at me forever, the same as if I told him I had a contagious disease or committed a horrible crime. I'd seen it with Lucas over the summer. I wouldn't be the same person to Jack. The girl he'd taught penny poker and challenged to bike races and shared a fort with in the maple tree would be gone. And I'd never be able to reclaim her.

And then there was that lady. The friend of the dead woman. How long would it be before I saw her again? Before she told her friends about me? Before one of them recognized me as Nan's granddaughter or the girl who lived next door to them?

When would they start showing up on my doorstep with torches? Overreaction? Maybe. Maybe not. It doesn't take much for a reputation to be built in a small town.

Figuring out how to use the mark required risks I couldn't take there. I needed a safe haven and I needed it to be Ashville. It's where my life was, my friends, my memories. It was home. That had to be preserved above all else so that maybe someday I could go back.

I'd written Jack a few times after I left; real letters, not e-mails. Nan always said an apology was best made in person, and if that wasn't possible, on fine stationery. I'd sent him the first letter right after I got here. Others over the following weeks.

Now I just texted. Short little notes, unable to fully sever the connection.

He never wrote back.

After rolling around in bed for an hour, the stuff with Jack and the scene with Zander fighting for space in my jittery brain, I called Tasha.

"H'lo?" Her voice was groggy. I glanced at the clock again, afraid I'd miscalculated, but 1:23 here meant after nine in Romania and Tash wasn't usually a late sleeper.

"Tasha? Hey, it's Cassie. Did I call too—"

"Cassie!" Hearing pre-caffeine Tasha's excitement made me smile. "How are you? I miss you! Wait!" I could almost see her doing the clock math. "Is everything okay? It must be . . ."

"The middle of the night," I finished. "It's fine. I just couldn't sleep and it finally seemed like a time I might actually catch you awake."

"Yeah . . . sort of. Late night."

We swapped stories about the usual stuff: the kids she was teaching English, my new school, her parents.

"You hear from anyone else at home?" I asked casually.

"Like who?" She was all innocence, totally onto me.

"I was just thinking about Jack," I said, still casual. Nothing wrong with asking about an old friend, right? "You know, wondered how he was . . ."

"Whether he was dating anyone? Asking about you?"

"Well, yeah."

She sighed. "I wish I could tell you, Cass, but I don't know. When I saw him last, he was pretty upset, couldn't understand why you left." She paused, asking carefully, "Why did you? I still feel like *I* don't know."

I closed my eyes, wishing I hadn't brought it up. "Oh, you know, Tash, it was just . . . being there with the memories of Nan . . ."

"Yeah, I know." I could tell she wasn't really buying it anymore. Just like Jack hadn't. "That's it, though? There wasn't anything else? Because . . ."

She didn't finish, just left it out there. "No, nothing else," I answered.

We talked a little more, but before we hung up Tasha circled back.

"You know, Cass, it was December when I saw him last." She

didn't even have to say his name. "Months ago," Tasha added for emphasis. "You know what they say about time, wounds, all of that. I wouldn't wait too long to get in touch."

"Yeah, maybe," I said. I hung up after our good-byes, not bothering to tell her how many times I'd tried.

I lay in bed for another half hour, but knew all chance of sleep was blown. I decided to go to the all-night diner two blocks away instead. I rarely went out this late, but when I wanted to, I could. It's one of the benefits of being my own boss at seventeen.

The diner was no-frills down to its very name: The Diner. I slid into an empty booth near the far corner after grabbing a job application for Liv. Not that I thought this was exactly what she had in mind, but I was here and they were "Now Hiring." I'd carefully folded it into my backpack and was flipping through a left-behind newspaper when the men's room door opened. I glanced up, without thought or expectation, immediately wishing myself back home in bed, sleepless or not.

The man walked toward me, lowered himself to his seat, and slurped at his coffee. He was lit with a soft, steady light. The last thing I needed tonight. The mark.

I glanced at the clock by the door: 2:47. He had less than twenty-one hours to live.

I closed my eyes, rubbing them as if I could erase his image: shaggy brown hair, worn flannel shirt, dirty jeans, heavy boots. He looked around fifty, but his scruffy face was tired, the kind that seems older than it is. Beaten down.

"What can I getcha, hon?" The waitress stood by my table. Behind her, I could see the man set down his cup and collect his things. I couldn't eat now anyway. I hated this feeling, hated what I had to do next: watch, learn, judge. Save him or don't? Trade a life for his? Without any evidence there even *was* a trade-off beyond the letter written by my long-dead and possibly crazy relative. Hardly rock-solid proof.

"Nothing," I told her, reaching heavily for my coat. "Changed my mind."

I slid out of the booth and followed him into the dark and freezing night.

The mark was as luminous as the moon against the near-black sky, more vivid than I'd ever seen it. I followed him, tense and anxious, staying in the shadows. But the man kept his head tucked against the wind that blew straight into us, never looking back, as we walked one block, then two, three, four from The Diner and my apartment. At the end of the last block, the man turned into an alley.

I hesitated, an ominous feeling stealing over me at the cusp of the dim passage. I'd never been to this part of Bellevue before. It was probably totally benign, if a little run down, during the day. But in the deserted night, it looked anything but safe.

What if his fate was to be mugged on his way home? What if following him made it my fate, too? What if *he* was the mugger; had known the whole time I was behind him and turned in here to trap me? What if *I* was his killer, protecting myself—his death the result of my own self-defense?

He'd gotten most of the way down the block while I stood paralyzed by my imagination. If he turned into a building or ducked down another street, I'd lose him.

And I couldn't lose him.

My hands clenched into fists, I started down the alley. I was within half a block of him when he paused, pulling out a set of keys and descending three stairs to a door. He unlocked it and slipped inside.

A light went on. I moved closer, crouching low, able to make out a sink, stove, and table. His kitchen. The counters held a toolbox, coffeemaker, and neatly stacked pile of magazines. It was frustratingly bland. No photos. No clutter or mess. No collection of empty booze bottles. Or guns or drugs or swastikas or signs saying "I'm a bad guy. Don't save me."

I waited, trying to ignore the bitter wind blowing through the corridor where I squatted, while he sifted through papers and envelopes. Finally he walked to the back room, turning on the light before disappearing into a bathroom.

I crept to the window, straining my eyes to see his nightstand where a photo caught my eye, the only personal thing I'd seen so far. It was a woman and a boy, I thought. The colors were washed out, but I couldn't tell if it was age or just a bad camera. And I couldn't discern at all who the people were, the woman equally likely to be his wife, girlfriend, or mother.

The man came back into the room then, wearing boxers and a T-shirt, and slid between his sheets, a book in hand. I watched for another minute, then sat back, thinking.

He'd made it safely home. Anything that might happen tonight—a stroke or heart attack—was probably beyond his or my ability to stop. There wasn't a chance I was knocking on his door at this hour anyhow.

I stood and edged carefully to the front of the house, checked the address, and ran back to my apartment, a plan having formed almost unconsciously in the time I'd spent watching him.

I flicked on the computer, changing into layers of my warmest clothes while it booted. I threw a flashlight and the binoculars *National Geographic* sent Petra into my backpack, then sat at the desk and typed in the address I'd repeated all the way home.

The reverse search came up with nine names, five of them men. After chucking the ones way too old or young, I was left with Mark Leventhall, 42, Peter McDaniels, 50, and Jackson Kennit, 48.

The computer's clock read 4:32. I'd already been gone nearly an hour. Quickly, I googled each name, jotting down key info and kicking myself for not taking an extra five seconds to look at the names on the mailboxes before running off. Two of these guys were a waste of time, but once I left the apartment I'd lose the chance to learn that Mark Leventhall was a newlywed or that Peter McDaniels worked in cancer research or—as the last search screen popped up—that Jackson Kennit had been arrested for drug possession three years ago. The things that might help me determine the value of his being here or gone.

Finally, I shoved the pages into my backpack and hustled back to his apartment. I had a pretty good idea who he was even before I saw his name—J. Kennit—freshly added to one of the building's three mailboxes.

I took a quick look in his window. He was still sleeping and still marked. Which meant he was still alive.

I pulled out the binoculars and trained them on the bedside photo. Definitely a woman and boy, about five or six years old with dark hair. Both were squinting into the sun. There was blue sky, grass, and absolutely nothing distinguishing about the landscape or way they were dressed. The picture could have been from forty years ago as easily as from last summer.

Slowly I panned the rest of the room, but there was little to see. It was unfair, but I was disappointed. Now that I knew his past, I'd hoped this would be a no-brainer. That there'd be a stash of powder-filled bags peeking out of the closet. But the apartment didn't look like an ex-con's drug den. It looked neat and clean; he looked clean, like a man on the mend.

I shoved the binoculars back in my bag and stood. Six forty-three. People might be up, getting ready for church soon. I walked back to the sidewalk, hoping there was somewhere to wait.

By ten the sun shone brightly, the temperature had hit thirty, and I'd learned what little I could from Jackson Kennit's neighbors.

By two I was exhausted and starting to wonder if maybe Jackson Kennit had already expired, though he was still marked every time I checked.

Finally, around two thirty he emerged, clean-shaven, neatly dressed in jeans and boots, and bundled into his jacket and scarf.

The anxiety and fear I'd felt on first seeing him at The Diner had dulled to glazed-eyed boredom over the past twelve sleepless hours, but when I saw him pass me they rushed back, jolting me upright. Jackson Kennit was awake, on the move, and still marked. He had less than ten hours to live. Unless I changed that.

I stumbled as I stood, my feet numb from so long in the biting air. I'd been ducking into a nearby store as often as possible but had still spent way too long outside.

Jackson Kennit didn't notice my odd, half-frozen gait, keeping his head low as he walked, just like the night before. I stayed close, aware that it could happen at any time—as he crossed the street, passed a dog or a precariously hung street sign. As always, I had no idea what kind of death I was waiting for.

Halfway down the block, he stopped and leaned against a post with a sign at the top. The bus his neighbors said he took to work. Weekend overtime at the machinery plant.

My heart sped up as my steps slowed down, the moments seeming longer and longer, like an old film whose projector has been shut off in midreel. I had a weird and awful sense of déjà vu. Of standing at another bus stop with another marked man. Robert

McKenzie. The one I'd followed when I'd first learned what the mark meant.

And suddenly I realized that my time with Jackson Kennit wasn't limited by the hours left in the day but by the minutes until he passed through the doors of Sterner's Manufacturing, because it seemed pretty unlikely they'd let some seventeen-year-old girl dressed like a bum trail him around at work. Just like I wouldn't have been allowed to follow Robert McKenzie into court or his office. Not that I'd needed to.

I watched Jackson Kennit, steps away from me, could see the small nick near his chin where the razor had cut too deep. He glanced up, maybe feeling my stare. His eyes were hooded, set under a heavy brow and purposely blank, like he was used to hiding things.

"Hi," I said, the word out before I realized it.

He studied me an extra second before answering. "Hi."

"Um . . . do you know if any of these buses go to the city?"

He shook his head. "Don't think so."

"Oh." Now what? I should ask something meaningful, get insight. I couldn't think of a thing. "Uh . . . well, is there somewhere good to eat around here?"

He frowned.

"I'm new to the neighborhood," I added.

"There's a diner down the street." He jerked his thumb toward where I'd first seen him. "'Bout five blocks away."

"Great. Thanks."

We stood in silence. Jackson Kennit shoved his hands in his pockets. Across the street a woman left an apartment building, carrying a baby in one arm and brown grocery bag in the other. She dropped her keys, juggling the baby and the bag to pick them up.

Jackson Kennit and I watched. "Should we help her?" I asked.
He shrugged. "Bus is coming."

It was. Two blocks down, it pulled away from the curb, lumbering toward us. The woman across the street glanced up, saw it, grabbed at the keys, then dropped the bag. The baby started crying.

"Hold the bus!" She waved to get our attention. "Don't let him leave."

Jackson Kennit said nothing so I yelled back, "Okay!"

I watched her thrust the keys into her pocket, stroke the baby's cheek, and give him a quick kiss before shoving two stray oranges back into her paper bag.

The bus pulled in front of me, blocking my view. The doors gasped open and Jackson Kennit climbed up, depositing his change. "There's a lady with a kid coming," I heard him tell the driver. "Think she needs to get on." Then he walked to his seat without a backward glance.

The driver stared at me expectantly, but the lady had rounded the front of the bus then, breathing hard.

"Go ahead." I waved her toward the door. "You first."

"Thanks so much," she said gratefully. "What a morning."

The woman hitched the baby higher, turning to fit herself and all her stuff through the doorway. I waited, hoping there'd still be a seat near Jackson Kennit. Behind him would be best. Once I worked up the nerve, I could just lean forward, quietly tell him what I knew, and urge him to go back home. I should have done it already, before he got any farther out into the world, but no one else on the bus was marked so I knew this ride, at least, was safe.

The woman mounted the stairs, the baby staring back at me over her shoulder. He waved, his hand covered with a brown-and-white mitten with ears. A cow. He still had a button nose and traces of roundness in his cheeks, but he was closer to two or three. Not really a baby. I could see the beginnings of his grown-up face in the shape of his brow, his pursed lips and bright, observant eyes. I could almost imagine what he'd look like at ten, or seventeen, or twenty-five.

If he made it that far.

And then they were gone, his mother still carrying him as she walked toward the rear of the bus where Jackson Kennit sat, his shoulder pressed against the window—a brown coat, outlined with a hazy light.

The driver looked at me, impatient now. "You coming or what?"

I hesitated, then shook my head. "No. Thanks."

He scowled and rolled his eyes, pulling the lever to fold the door closed.

I watched the bus, cruising slowly, farther and farther down the street, feeling scared and empty, not fully believing that I'd just done it. I'd let him go.

I'd never see Jackson Kennit again, this man I didn't know but had spent the night with. By tomorrow, he'd be gone. I wanted to run after him, couldn't shake the way he'd looked down at me from his elevated seat as the bus rolled past, like the truth had somehow suddenly dawned on him as he watched me watching him drive away.

But what if it was that little boy's life—and all the possibility in it—that I traded for?

That's what had stopped me.

It made me sick to think of it because it might not be a little boy who I'd saved. It might be someone much worse, someone who didn't deserve or want it at all. Like the old man on the bench or Eduard Sanchez, the man I'd warned in Kansas who killed his wife.

Or it might be no one at all.

I might have let Jackson Kennit die for nothing.

I walked home, freezing, exhausted in body and otherwise, wishing this day away and fighting off the dark and suffocating guilt that was trying to worm its way in.

I focused on the only thing I could—the tiny bit of hope that Demetria could help me make sense of what I'd just done and what I was supposed to do the next time. Because that was the one sure thing: there would be a next time. I just hoped I had some answers by then.

chapter 9

I slept most of the rest of Sunday and a good part of Monday too, calling in sick to the funeral home and skipping school. I had a huge calc test, but there's no way I could get my head into it.

"How're you feeling?" Petra asked, flopping onto a chair, still in uniform after her Monday shift.

"Better," I said, though I wasn't really. I didn't have a cold, like I'd told her, just a chill that felt like it might never leave. I'd already thrown out the newspaper that told me about the accident at the machine shop yesterday.

"How was the loony bin?" I asked.

"Awesome."

"I'm going tomorrow." I couldn't live like this, not knowing, toying with people's lives. I needed answers.

"You know, Cassie, I've been thinking." Petra eyed me carefully. "I'm not sure your going to see her—this Demetria—is really such a good idea."

I kept my face blank, refusing to show the panic edging in. "What do you mean?"

She shrugged uncomfortably. "I saw your name in the file, just a small note, that you'd raised your voice with her. Not a big deal on its own," she added quickly, seeing I was about to butt in with explanations and excuses. "It's not just that, though. When you talk about her after your visits you seem . . ." She bit her lip, thinking. "I don't know. Kind of empty? I'm just not sure you're really going to get anything out of it. Not what you're looking for, at least. I mean, she's not your mother; she clearly has problems that your mother didn't . . ." Petra stopped and I could almost see her picking through what she remembered of my mom's hospital records. She'd been the psychiatrist on duty when I'd gone looking for them. The one who told me my mom committed suicide, read me the notes about her "delusions." It was pretty awful stuff and I think it weighed on Petra, made her feel, in some part, responsible. Especially since, as she told me after we moved here, her mom had spent time in a mental hospital too.

"I can understand your wanting to connect and find some kind of closure—believe me, I *know* how you're feeling—but if closure exists, I don't know, this might not be the best place to find it."

No, I thought, it's the *only* place to find it. I forced myself to stay calm, keeping my voice firm and measured, the best way to convince Petra. "I know Demetria's not my mother, but maybe she's enough like her to teach me something. I didn't really raise my voice to her," I said. "Not in a mean way. She was with me and then she wasn't, you know? I was just trying to get her back, keep her attention."

"Yeah." Petra nodded sympathetically. "I totally understand how frustrating that can be. But it's like that a lot with the patients." Petra sighed. "Maybe I'm not expressing it very well," she said. "I just see you holding on to this too tightly, hoping for too much . . ."

"And you don't want me to be disappointed."

"Right."

"I won't be," I said, knowing full well that I would—*devastated* might be more accurate—if I didn't get what I needed from Demetria. But I told Petra what she wanted to hear. "I get it that Demetria's case is different from my mother's, but . . ." I shrugged. "You know, sometimes when I'm there, I think about my mom spending the last four years of her life at the Barrow Center without many visitors, maybe thinking no one cared or wondering why Nan or I never came. Even if I'm not learning about my mom from Demetria, I feel like it's still helping. Like maybe I'm making up for the things I wasn't able to do for my mother, in some kind of roundabout karmic way. You know?"

Petra smiled cautiously. "Okay. I just want to be sure you're not pinning too much on learning what your mom was like by visiting this girl. From what I can see, there's about as much that's different about her and your mom as there is that's the same."

"Right. Don't worry, Petra. It's all good."

As long as one of the similarities was the one I was looking for.

I had no luck with Demetria the next day, though. I felt like we were in reverse, actually, unable to even get her to make eye contact. Patience, I kept telling myself, remembering Petra's warning.

Between her and Jackson Kennit and exhaustion, I'd been a virtual ghost in the hallways at Franklin Parris High.

"Where the hell have you been, Renfield?" Liv demanded when she finally caught up with me by my locker on Thursday.

"What do you mean?" I looked up at her innocently, but it felt so fake I quickly busied myself rearranging my books.

"It's like you've been avoiding me." Liv turned her head, sniffing her armpit. "Do I smell bad?"

I smiled. "No, Liv. Sorry. I've been busy this week, extra hours at work and stuff."

"Uh-huh. Dead people are better company than I am, huh?"

"Yeah, something like that." I *had* been ducking out, spending lunch in the library and purposely taking paths through school that would keep me away from Liv, Hannah, and Erin. And Zander. They were all too much of a distraction. Jackson Kennit had been a bleak reminder that I needed to focus on what I'd come here for: finding answers.

"Well," Liv said, "I'd been hoping you'd share some of that expertise with me yesterday, but you were MIA so I went without you."

"Went where?"

"To the funeral."

For a second, I thought she was talking about Jackson Kennit's funeral, which the obituary had said was on Wednesday. Yesterday. I'd considered going. It would have been the right move researchwise, but I wasn't ready to face his people. It was one thing to study mourners at Ludwig & Wilton and try to figure out how things might be different for them, but doing that with the family of someone I saw the mark on and decided to let die? Way too close. I couldn't go there yet. Not on my first one.

But I still had no idea what Liv was talking about. "Whose funeral?"

She looked at me like I had two heads. "Where have you been, Cass? Really. If I hadn't seen you practically running down the hall away from me yesterday, I'd say you'd been cutting classes. Nick Altos's dad died Sunday. His funeral was yesterday. We all went. You know Nick—quiet? From my art class? We talked to him at the mall that night . . ." She shook her head. "You were probably too wrapped up playing touchy-feely with Zander Dasios."

But I did remember, the guy from Loserville. My heart sank, thinking of the photo by the bedside. The boy with dark hair. Like Nick's. "What was his name?" I asked faintly.

"Who? His dad?"

I nodded.

"Jack Kennit. Jackson, actually. Kind of a cool name, right?"

Oh shit.

"Renfield? You okay? For someone who works around dead people, you look a little freaked out."

Way more than a little. "They have different names."

"Who?" Liv frowned. "Nick and his dad? Yeah. It's called divorce. Happens a lot these days."

"Uh-huh," I said dully. "So what happened?" I knew already, of course, but I let Liv rattle on about the accident, his drug history, and everything else, giving me time to get it together.

At the end of her explanation, I asked what I needed—and dreaded—to know. "How's Nick?"

"A total wreck. How would you be?" Liv shifted her weight, glancing down the hallway. "He was back in school today. I'm not sure I would have been."

"No," I said. "Me neither."

Nick Altos's dad. It could only be worse if it were someone like Liv or Tasha. I wondered how often Nick had seen his father, what they'd done or said to each other the last time.

I had a feeling I'd find out soon enough. I didn't want to do it like this: hear the regrets of someone I knew and ask the questions about how life might have changed if only I'd made a different decision. But I had to, like it or not.

chapter 10

Liv had wanted me to come over and help with her Lit paper, but I begged off.

"You sure I don't smell?" she'd asked, mock sniffing her armpit again.

I smiled, not quite able to pull it off. "Positive, Liv." I shrugged. "Can't keep the dead waiting." We made plans to go job hunting the next afternoon instead. I gave her the application for The Diner, feeling nauseated just looking at it. When I picked it up, Nick's dad was still alive. Sitting in a booth. Drinking coffee. Now he was as dead as whoever I'd be working on at the funeral home.

Mr. Ludwig already had the body on the table by the time I scrubbed up and came in.

"Feeling better?" he asked without looking up. I saw him delicately slide an arterial tube into the woman's neck. The carotid artery was the injection point for chemicals that flowed through the body, pushing its natural fluids out the jugular vein that ran alongside it. My first embalming had been a fast and repulsive lesson on the circulatory system.

"Yes, thanks," I answered, trying to be totally cool with the blue-gray hue of the woman's skin, which hung limp as the sheet draped over her lower half. I wondered if I'd ever get used to this. Embalming was the absolute worst part of mortuary work. I could've told Mr. Ludwig I didn't want to do it—I think he knew it was a struggle for me—but I wasn't a quitter so I gutted it out. No pun intended.

Mr. Ludwig stepped back and, satisfied that the ligature was secure, turned the dials and knobs that started the formaldehyde and other chemicals. I wandered to the counter, flipping through the lady's funeral program. Standard-issue stuff: pictures of her with her husband on a cruise ship, surrounded by her kids at a barbecue, an old posed family portrait. The quote was by Emily Dickinson: "Unable are the loved to die. For love is immortality." I liked that one.

"She wasn't religious?" I asked Mr. Ludwig. They usually used biblical quotes.

He shrugged. "The burial's at St. Matthew's."

Catholic. But maybe not very devout. "I was doing some reading this weekend," I told him, ignoring the stealthy hum of the machine. "I never realized how many people believe in reincarnation instead of heaven and hell." Almost a quarter of the world population, according to Ryan's books.

He gave a quick nod. "Of course. Nearly all of India, Japan, China—the Eastern religions—believe the soul returns in some form, bettering itself until it's reached enlightenment."

I'd thought about Jackson Kennit during my reading, of course. Had I sent him to be reanimated in a new body? Or was he burning in hell because I hadn't warned him to confess? Which was the truth? What had he believed? And what did it mean if his beliefs were the wrong ones, and reality was different from what he'd built his faith on?

"Do you believe in reincarnation?" I asked Mr. Ludwig.

"It's what I was taught." He twirled the scalpel gently between his fingers, waiting for this first stage of the embalming to finish. "It's what my mother believes."

"But do *you*?"

Mr. Ludwig pursed his already-thin lips, the barest of lines across his face while he thought. "Truthfully, I'm not sure what I believe, Cassie," he said finally. "Death is the simplest act shrouded by the greatest mystery. Any of the scenarios seem equally likely and unlikely to me. It's like asking about the chicken and the egg. The question is unanswerable because its truth can't be tested."

"Deep," I said, smiling faintly.

Mr. Ludwig glanced up and smiled too, his face merry again. "It is, isn't it? But that's the essence of religion: faith. Believing in something that cannot be confirmed." He walked around the table, massaging the woman's arm to break up a blockage.

My eyes traveled to her face, wrinkled, without color or definition, beyond gender or emotion. Was she watching us from heaven? Starting life anew in a different body? Or was this all there was?

"What do you believe?" Mr. Ludwig asked, as if reading my thoughts.

Nan and I never really talked about religion when I was growing up, almost purposely avoiding it, it seemed now, though I wasn't aware of it at the time. I had vague ideas of heaven and hell, but nothing that could really be called a belief. Certainly nothing I'd stake my life—or someone else's—on.

"I guess I believe we should do the best we can with our time here since there's no way to know what happens next," I said finally.

Mr. Ludwig paused, the barest trace of a smile still on his face. "Yes." He nodded slowly. "Just so."

I ran into Ryan as I was leaving the prep room. Literally. He was charging down the short hallway, a cardboard box in front of his face, and I smacked right into him.

"Jesus," he muttered, rubbing his elbow and stooping to pick up the packages of gloves, face masks, and other stuff that had toppled out of the box.

"Sorry," I said, bending down to help. "I didn't see you."

"Yeah. Got that," he answered, looking not at all amused.

We tossed the packages back into the box in silence. I watched Ryan, my head still bent. He wasn't hot like Zander, but definitely cute and interesting. Engaging rather than enticing. I liked him, though I couldn't decide how much. "I've been reading the books you left me," I said.

"Oh yeah?" He glanced up and I caught a quick half smile before he reached for a roll of cotton.

"Interesting stuff."

"Like what?" Ryan sat back on his heels, crossing his arms as if daring me to come up with something. Like a teacher giving a pop quiz.

"Well . . . like how the Baha'i of Iran bury their dead within an hour's travel of the spot where they died. And how Jehovah's Witnesses believe only 144,000 of them can go to heaven. I mean, what a raw deal for virtuous soul number 144,001, right?"

He laughed.

I continued. "And the Tibetan Buddhist monks do some pretty

strange stuff to their dead that is, uh . . . very different from what we do here."

Ryan was grinning, his eyes—the gray-blue of rain clouds—amused. "That's what you took away from it, huh?"

"Well," I said, "not only that." I'd just thought the weird stuff might impress him more. I told him the things Mr. Ludwig and I had talked about.

"What religion are you?" I asked as we walked down the hall toward the supply room, items now stacked haphazardly back in his box.

"Protestant. But I've studied lots of them," he added. "Gone to different churches. Testing them out, you know?"

"Yeah," I said slowly, "I do." It was an idea I'd been toying with for a while. "Listen," I said impulsively, not certain I wanted him along, but knowing if I had a partner and was committed to a day and time, I'd really go. "I've actually been thinking I'd like to do that. Would you want to, you know, come with me?"

Ryan shrugged like it was nothing, but I could tell he was pleased. "Sure. What'd you have in mind?"

"Well, I was thinking of starting with my church, my people's that is. Greek Orthodox. Maybe this Sunday?"

He nodded. "We'll have to come here straight after."

"I know. The Rubin burial."

"Right."

We stood there awkwardly, then spoke at the same time.

"So, I'll meet you . . . ," I said, while Ryan said, "Should I pick you . . . ?"

We stopped and I hoped this wouldn't be a mistake. I worried that he might be too eager, that he might like me and think I liked him too—which I did, but maybe not in that way.

But I'd already asked him to go.

"How about we meet here?" I suggested, all business. "Then we can leave our work stuff in the lockers."

"Do you know what time the service is?"

"Nine." I'd done the research, just never motivated to actually go.

"And it's about an hour and a half till we get back and all."

"Yeah, I figure it'll be just enough time." We were both scheduled at eleven to prep for the service.

"Okay," he agreed, smiling. "Yeah, great."

chapter 11

After much deliberation, Liv decided to focus her job search on Addison, the town center closest to her house. She stopped by The Diner, but without experience they'd only hire her to bus tables for minimum wage. Not quite what she'd hoped for. There were a few restaurants in Addison and a strip of stores, so it made sense to keep looking and was better than going to the mall, though there'd still be too many people for my liking. It was hard to imagine where she could apply that there wouldn't be too many people. Other than Ludwig & Wilton, of course.

"Did you tell your parents?" I asked as we sped down Chestnut Street, away from school. I checked my seat belt to be sure it was tight.

"Yeah," Liv said. "They didn't say I couldn't."

"But . . . ?"

She shrugged. "My mom was like, 'You don't need to do that, we have plenty of money' and 'you should focus on school, there'll be plenty of time to work later.'"

"Right. Well, you expected that."

"She wasn't as unreasonable as usual," Liv said. "Which makes me think that maybe the 'we have plenty of money' part wasn't totally true." She sighed. "I wish they'd just tell me the whole story instead of protecting me, you know?"

"Yup. I sure do."

"Either way, it can't hurt for me to earn my own spending money," Liv continued, barely pausing at an intersection. *Stoptional*, she'd told me. They'd put up a traffic light if they *really* wanted you to stop. "I just don't feel right about asking them for it now. Plus, I think I just kind of want a job." She turned the corner, glancing over. "Does that make me weird?"

"You're asking *me* if you're weird?"

"Right." Liv crossed her eyes and stuck out her tongue. "What am I thinking?"

"I don't think it's weird at all," I said, smiling. "I really like working."

"And considering I'll be working with people who are actually alive, I should love it."

"Exactly," I said. "It's kind of nice to have that something else that's not school and not home." And not Nick or his dad or death, I thought. I felt a little guilty, like I was taking an unapproved day off, going job hunting with Liv instead of concentrating on my "gift." But now that I was here, talking about normal things, I realized how much I needed a break.

"Did you work before you came here?" she asked.

"Just over the summer, when I lived in Kansas."

Liv turned into the parking lot behind the town's strip of stores. "At a funeral parlor?"

"Nope. Coffee shop."

"Uh-huh." She zipped up the row of spaces so fast I closed my eyes, afraid to watch the pedestrian sure to become like windshield bug splat. The car swung hard right and jerked to a stop. We were in a spot. Liv killed the engine and asked, "So what on earth made you decide to work where you do now?"

I bit my lip, my mind racing for an answer. "The customers are a lot less cranky?" I said finally.

Liv snorted. "Maybe you should have made stronger coffee instead."

We went to the three restaurants first and all of them gave her the same spiel. No experience, no job.

"The stores are going to say the same thing," she said, disappointed.

"Maybe. But let's check it out. Persistence, Liv."

She trailed behind me, enthusiasm waning as we picked up an application and lukewarm reception at Carey's, Zapatos, and Ever After. And then I had a brainstorm. "What about TREND?" I asked. "We should *totally* go there. You love that place."

"They will never hire me, Cassie," she said. "Are you kidding? I'm sure their people have been doing it for, like, years."

"But you're a complete natural for them. Not like these places." I waved toward Ever After's flowery purple storefront.

"Maybe . . . ," she said, totally unconvinced.

We got back in the car and I talked her into going to TREND anyway. It'd be a longer drive, maybe another ten miles from her house, nestled between a yogurt shop and dry cleaner near the highway entrance, but it was so perfect for Liv that she couldn't *not* try. I couldn't believe I hadn't thought of it earlier. It was one of her favorite stores, with a quirky and expensive vintage vibe. She might be right about the experience thing, but I hoped they'd look past that because Liv had an amazing eye for style. She'd completely reorganized my closet one day when we were hanging out, hiding all the orange stuff in the back. "You should *not* wear that color," she said. "It makes you look jaundiced. And also, I've been meaning to tell you that this skirt"—she held up my favorite kilt—"would look way better with something like this"—tight black T-shirt—"than that baggy sweater you always wear it with."

"Don't hold back, Liv. Tell me what you really think."

She shrugged, grinning. "If you'd rather look like a sack of potatoes . . ."

"No, no," I said. "Honesty is welcome here. Even if I love that sweater. And orange." But I knew she was right.

We parked just to the left of TREND's front window so she wouldn't feel like I was staring at her through the plate glass. I waited in the car after a "hold your head high, be confident, you look awesome" pep talk, crossing my fingers that I hadn't just sent her to have her last bit of job confidence shredded. She came out ten minutes later grinning.

"They don't usually hire without experience, but the manager was totally cool. She dug my glasses and remembered me shopping there. I have an interview Monday!"

"That's awesome, Liv!" I said, breathing a huge internal sigh of relief. "I've got a good feeling about this."

"Me too. Ice cream to celebrate?"

"Absolutely!"

We settled for frozen yogurt, neither of us feeling like trekking to Ben & Jerry's at the mall. I told her what my job interview in Kansas had been like, she asked what she should wear—as if I had any clue—and then she started in on Ryan.

"I'm actually seeing him this weekend," I admitted. "Outside work."

"Oooh! A date!"

"It is *so* not a date, Liv. We're going to church."

She nodded approvingly. "That's very sensible, Cassandra. Show that boy exactly what kind of wholesome, God-fearing girl you are."

"Ha, ha."

"Well." She licked her spoon, then swooped it around the sides, scraping up the final mouthfuls. "I'm glad you're taking my advice at least."

"Which was . . . ?" I knew what it was but I wanted to hear his name. And anything else she might say about him.

"Duh. To stay away from Zander Dasios. *Obviously.* I'll bet he wouldn't go to church with you."

"Probably not." But I couldn't help wondering what it'd be like if he did. If we stood side by side, arms brushing occasionally. My cheeks flushed.

"You're thinking about him," she said in a singsong voice.

"I'm not."

"Liar," Liv said matter-of-factly, shoveling the last spoonful of strawberry yogurt into her mouth.

"I was thinking about going to church."

"Mm-hmm," Liv said, smirking as she stood, her empty bowl in hand. "Church always makes me all red in the face too."

chapter 12

The closest Greek Orthodox church was ten miles away, coinciden-
tally in Demetria's school district. I'd been surprised when Petra
said she was so close to us—I guess I expected her to live near the
hospital in the city—and it made me wonder again about her and
Zander. Did he know her? Was it really him I saw at Vauxhall?
The idea of the two of them—knowing she was pregnant—stirred
up all kinds of weird emotions, none of them pleasant.

Ryan was waiting on the steps of the funeral home. I figured
we'd take the bus to the church since that's how I always got around,
but Ryan looked at me like I was nuts when I mentioned it.

"No, I'll drive," he said.

"You have a car?"

He smiled, very amused. "Where are you from exactly?"

I felt my face grow warm. Of course he had a car. Liv's friend
told her his house was huge. Death must be very profitable. Then
again, I had plenty of money too, thanks to Nan. A car just seemed
like a hassle I didn't need.

I shrugged. "I've just never seen you driving. You're always already here. I guess I assumed you got around the same way I do. My bad."

Turned out Ryan has a very nice car, low and sporty, with soft tan leather seats and butt warmers. He turned on both mine and his as we got in.

"You see my dad and Mr. Ludwig in there?" he asked, pulling smoothly away from the curb.

"Yeah, but I just tossed my stuff in the locker and left. Do they know we're . . . going to church?"

"Together?" He smiled, reading into my hesitation. "I don't think so. Does it matter?"

"No." And yes. I still felt a little weird about being here with him, blurring the lines between work and whatever this was, but Ryan seemed completely at ease. Maybe I was overthinking things. I changed the subject. "So what do your friends think about your job?"

He laughed. "They think it's weird. Also bizarre, morbid, gross, you name it." Ryan shrugged. "Doesn't really bother me. I can't imagine doing the stuff they do to earn money—working at the mall or McDonald's or whatever. So boring."

"I totally agree." Liv would love TREND, but it wasn't for me. For a variety of reasons.

He glanced over, still grinning. "Death is fascinating, isn't it?"

"You know," I said, "saying stuff like that will only make your friends think you're more bizarre."

"Do you think I'm bizarre?"

"Yes."

His grin got bigger. "But you're okay with that."

"I asked you to church, didn't I?"

"Maybe you're trying to reform me."

"Yup," I said, smiling now too. "You got me."

Ryan talked about school, a bike race he was training for, college plans for next year. He was decidedly normal, despite his preoccupation with death. Kind of like me.

We hurried through a packed parking lot and made it into church five minutes before the service started. Inside, the air was thick with musky incense. And warm. Bodies filled nearly every row all the way to the railing between them and the raised altar backed by a wall of gold-leaf icons.

I felt a hundred eyes on me as we walked down the aisle, slipping into the first empty space about halfway down.

The ceremony started, voices drifting solemnly through the church, priests in heavy robes chanting as they walked slow, measured steps, swinging a golden ball that leaked perfumed smoke as they went.

I'd read about this in Ryan's books the night before. The incense symbolized prayers rising to God. Lots of prayers, it seemed. Greek Orthodoxy is a branch of the Catholic church, with many of the same beliefs and sacraments. There are small differences like the incense, use of icons instead of statues, and, more significant, the absence of purgatory. It's either straight to heaven or hell for the Greeks.

The part I was *really* interested in, of course, was how the shift from gods and goddesses to a single God happened; one myth traded for another. Sixteen hundred years ago, the emperor declared the Greeks' religion—what we call mythology—illegal, I'd read, punishable by fines, imprisonment, and death.

It'd be like me telling Ryan the sky was red, and if he didn't believe it, I'd kill him. He'd probably agree it was red, even pass it on to his children so they'd be safe. His children would repeat it to theirs and so on until one day everyone in the world believed the sky was red.

Doesn't mean it is. Just like it doesn't mean the myths weren't true.

I scanned the crowd around me, people chanting in unison. Whatever their history, they definitely seemed to believe the sky was red now.

And then I saw him, across the church, two rows behind, alone, not chanting, and staring right at me.

Definitely not a look-alike. Zander.

He winked.

I turned my head, quickly enough that Ryan looked over. "You okay?" he whispered.

I nodded, feeling my face burn, and fixed my eyes on the prayer book, though it was impossible to focus on the words or the service. I'd been avoiding Zander at school in a passive-aggressive sort of way: forcing myself not to look toward his locker, but still walking past that hall. Purposely facing the other way at lunch, aware of him behind me the whole time. We hadn't spoken since that night outside the theater and I knew I needed to concentrate on Demetria and figuring out the mark, but I was having a hard time erasing the memory of us standing inches apart, my hair tangled around his fingers the way he seemed twisted throughout my thoughts. He was everywhere I was, even when—as at Vauxhall—he really wasn't. I didn't want to want him. But I did. I couldn't help it.

I was on edge the rest of the service, not allowing myself to look back at Zander and overly aware of Ryan beside me. I still didn't know exactly what I thought of Ryan, but I knew I didn't want to face Zander with him there.

We filed out of the church at the end way too slowly. I kept waiting for Zander's approach, willing myself invisible. Ryan noticed.

"Why so jumpy?"

"I'm not jumpy," I said, glancing to the left.

"No?"

When we reached the foyer, Ryan turned up his collar against the cold and decided to let it be. "C'mon," he said, tugging gently on my sleeve, ready to weave through the final press of people. "We've gotta hurry or we'll be stuck in this parking lot forever."

chapter 13

I finally got up the nerve to approach Nick Altos on Tuesday. After days of watching him slink through the halls, I walked into the library and saw him alone at one of the tables in back. It was kismet.

I pretended to look at the volumes shelved behind him, mostly on the human body, which I'd seen quite enough of at work. Nick was reading a magazine, something about electronics, pinching at his lips from time to time, deep in thought. His dark hair was shaggy, but his jeans and gray long-sleeved tee were clean and neat. I felt a small relief that he looked more or less normal, holding it together pretty well.

I grabbed a book and slid into the chair across from him. "Okay if I sit here?"

He looked up and his eyes showed what his clothes masked: a deep, hooded melancholy. Nick shrugged, returning to his magazine, but his concentration was broken. I decided not to let him get it back.

"Nick?"

He looked up, surprised.

"I just wanted to say I heard about your dad and I'm really sorry."

He frowned. "What do you care? You didn't know him, don't know me."

I nodded, trying not to be bruised by his anger. "My grand-mother died last year," I said. "I lived with her after my parents passed away when I was little. You're right, I don't know you, but I remember how hard it was for me right after." Nick was looking down and I couldn't tell at all how he was feeling. "Anyway, I just wanted to say I'm sorry. And I think you're brave to be back here so soon."

I held my breath, hoping he wouldn't freak out on me.

"Where else would I be?" he muttered. "Not much good sit-ting around the house."

It was a small opening. "Yeah, that's kind of the conclusion I came to also," I said carefully.

His head still bent, Nick reached up and wiped angrily at his eyes.

"Were you close to him?" I all but whispered it. Partly because we were in the library, but more because I was afraid I was way overstepping my bounds. I wasn't even sure Nick knew my name.

He didn't respond. I was pretty sure he'd heard me, but when a minute passed and still nothing, I wondered if I was wrong. "Nick . . ."

His head snapped up and he glared at me. "I heard you."

I winced. "Sorry, I just . . ." I had no idea what to say. I was afraid I'd blown it.

Nick's eyes cut away from me as the librarian walked past, her arms loaded with books for reshelving. When he turned back, his expression was blank. "I hung up on him the last time he called," he said bluntly.

I waited.

"I'm sure you've heard. He was a deadbeat. A druggie, thief, no-good bastard. That's what my mom's said for years." Nick looked down, quiet for a few seconds, then quickly wiped a sleeve across his face.

"But he was still your dad," I said.

He looked back at me, his eyes teary. "Yeah." Nick took a ragged breath. "He was still my dad."

"Someone said he'd gone through rehab . . ."

Nick snorted. "About seven times."

"It never stuck?"

"Nope," Nick said, adding softly, "never will now." He paused, studying his hands as he said, "I used to daydream about what it would be like if he'd ever, you know, stayed clean." He shook his head. "Not sure what the point of that was."

"Maybe just thinking good things about him?"

Nick's face smoothed a little. "Yeah." He nodded. "Maybe."

"What was he like?"

"When he was clean? Great. Fun. When he was off the wagon? Not so much," Nick said flatly.

"Did you ever feel . . . I don't know . . . like there was anything different this time? That the rehab might stick?" I asked it fast, hoping he wouldn't think too hard about why I was probing the way no normal person would. But I could tell his thoughts were somewhere else.

Nick bit his lip self-consciously before answering. "My mom says I'm hopelessly hopeful about him. It's okay, as long as I don't kid myself about what he did to us." I could almost hear his mom's voice, harsh, no longer the sunny-faced woman in Jackson Kennit's bedside photo. "But I don't know. There *was* something different this time. He was working. Not just for a week or two, but for months. He had an apartment . . ." Nick trailed off.

I thought about that tidy apartment, the way Jackson Kennit had gone home, gone to bed, gone to work. A responsible, ordinary life. Probably not so ordinary for a former addict. I wanted to tell Nick that and how his dad had held the bus for the lady and her son coming across the street, maybe thinking about his own son. But, of course, I couldn't.

"My mom was probably right," he said dismissively.

I looked across the table, the pain so clear on Nick's face, and had to blink to keep my own tears back. I had made him feel this way. I let his dad die. And for what? Some crazy idea that if I saved him a little boy might die in his place?

"This might not help much," I started, straining to keep my voice steady. I needed to offer him something, some small atonement. "But I think it's okay to believe the best about people, especially after they're gone. I didn't know your dad, but I bet he loved you and, however your last conversation with him went, I bet he knew you loved him, too."

Nick was silent and I winced, sure he was going to ream me out for going off like I was some kind of authority on his feelings or his dad's. A minute that felt like a hundred passed quietly and I finally hazarded a glance up.

He was biting his lip again and looking down at the table.

I stood, collecting my things as quickly and smoothly as I could, my face burning with shame and guilt.

I had taken only a step, on tiptoes, wishing for an invisibility cloak, when Nick said, "Hey."

He reached out and his hand brushed my arm so lightly I saw rather than felt his touch whisper across the sleeve of my sweater. His eyes held mine for just the second it took him to say "Thanks."

I nodded and left him alone at the table, wishing I felt like I deserved it.

I trudged through the rest of the day in a funk, barely able to be glad when it was over. Liv found me at one point, bounding down the hall, positively giddy. TREND had just called—she'd gotten the job. I forced a smile and congrats. Fortunately, she was too excited to notice how weak both were.

I'd taken my cell out of my backpack after leaving Nick at the library, thinking I'd text Jack. It was purely instinct. I couldn't really tell him why I was upset, even if I felt desperately that he might be the one person whose reassurance could help me feel less like a monster. The delicate weight of the phone pulled on my pocket now as I stood by my locker after last bell, mindlessly wrapping a scarf around my neck. I didn't even notice Zander standing two feet away until the kid next to me, some freshman with shiny braces, slammed his door shut and clomped off.

"Hey," Zander said, leaning casually against the wall of lockers.

My heart could hardly muster an extra *thump-thump*. He was hot as ever, but the weight of what I'd done to Nick sapped me of the patience for boy-girl games. "Hey." I shrugged on my wool coat and nudged the locker door closed.

"I saw you at church with your boyfriend."

I looked up at him and frowned. This was exactly the kind of b.s. I wasn't in the mood for. "He's not my boyfriend."

"No?" A small smile teased the corners of Zander's lips.

"No," I answered firmly. "We work together. He's a friend."

"Hmm," Zander said, rubbing his jaw thoughtfully, looking smug and superior. "I wonder if he'd say the same thing."

I didn't answer. This was a pointless conversation that I wasn't going to prolong. I turned my back on him and started walking.

"So," he said, trailing me down the hall. "What were you doing at my church?"

"The same thing as you," I said, not looking at him. "Singing, praying, kneeling. You know, worshipping God and all."

"Yes. I saw that," he said, taking two long strides and stepping in front of me, so that I almost bumped into him. "What I meant is: why? You don't go to my church."

I crossed my arms, staring up at him and hating the way my pulse raced even though he was appallingly arrogant. "How do you know? Maybe you've just never seen me there before."

"Oh, my mistake. So do you go to my church?"

"No." I flushed slightly. "But I *am* Greek. It *is* the kind of church I'd go to. You don't own the rights to it, you know."

I started walking again, maneuvering around Zander, who neatly stepped to the side and matched my pace. He walked uncomfortably close. Or maybe too comfortably close. "Didja like it?"

I shot him a quick, wary look, but it seemed like a genuine question. "It was interesting," I said, electing a genuine answer. "I didn't notice anyone with you. Do you go alone?"

"Sometimes," Zander answered vaguely. "How was it interesting?"

"Well . . ." I didn't know much about Zander, but people are touchy about their beliefs, even people you'd never expect to care. "There was a good feeling," I told him carefully, realizing only as I spoke how true it was. "In the group, the community, I guess. It felt . . . comfortable, like I belonged, kind of."

"Mm-hmm."

"I've never spent much time with Greeks. Back in Pennsylvania, you know, it was just me and my grandmother. She didn't go to church..." I was rambling. Like an idiot. "Anyway," I said, more decisively, "that part was nice."

"But . . . ?"

"Well, some of the ceremony and the outfits and the church itself, the . . . decorations or whatever you call it . . ."

"The icons? The gold? The crosses?"

"Yeah, all of that. It's a bit much."

"You think?" He smiled impishly and I couldn't help but smile back. His grin made me feel warm and a little light-headed, the way I'd always felt around Jack, except that there was something protective about Jack. Zander felt nearly the opposite of safe.

"Do you go every week?" I asked, waving as we passed Erin at her locker. She stared at us, her eyebrows raised.

"No," Zander said. "Only when I feel like it."

"Isn't that a sin?" The Orthodox, like the Catholics, were strict about the rituals.

"I suppose it is," he said, smirking devilishly. "Certainly not my first."

I couldn't tell if it was just me or if everything he said was laced with innuendo, but my face felt too hot again. We'd reached the doors at the end of the hall that led to the rear exit of the school. I heard them rattle, felt the chilled air through the crack, and tightened my coat around me. "Well," I said, giving Zander a quick smile. "I'll see you."

"Let me give you a ride home."

"Oh, that's okay," I said way more casually than I felt. "Thanks, though." I took a step toward the door, already knowing he wasn't going to let me go.

"What? Are you afraid of me?"

There was a playfulness in his voice, but something else underneath. Something that told me maybe I *should* be afraid. Of the way people talked about him, the things they called him. Demetria flashed, unwarranted, in my thoughts. "Should I be?" I faced him, folding my arms across my chest.

His eyes were locked on mine and, though he was smiling, it seemed false, his real feelings and thoughts kept somewhere deeper, where I suspected very few people were allowed. "What would you be afraid of?" he asked softly.

It struck me as a bigger question, as if he meant in the totality of the universe, not fears about him, but about life.

Before I could answer, Zander said, "C'mon." He walked past me, turning to wait at the door. "It's freezing out. Way too cold to walk."

I hesitated for one more second, Demetria caught in my mind, not because I thought he was involved with her, but because it had just occurred to me that maybe he knew her. For real. From church or something. And if he did, he could tell me things about her that might help. That was all the excuse I really needed.

"Okay." I shrugged, following him to the door and forgetting to ask how he knew that I walked to school.

chapter 14

If I'd had to guess, I would have put Zander behind the wheel of some fancy low-slung Italian sportscar—sleeker and more danger-ous than Ryan's. Instead, it was a banged-up, dark-blue Nissan. I guess Zander's father didn't own a thriving funeral home. Or maybe he did, for all I knew about Zander, which was basically nothing.

He opened the door for me, waving his hand grandly at the passenger seat. I smiled and climbed in as gracefully as I could.

His car was neat, freshly vacuumed, and smelled intoxicatingly like him, earthy and Eastern, like incense and patchouli oil. The scent was faint, the way wood like cedar or pine smells, its fra-grance essential rather than applied.

Zander got in, cranking the heat up full blast and unwrapping his scarf. A small gold charm on a black leather necklace flashed in the dome light as he leaned forward. It settled against his silky olive skin in the spot where his top shirt button was undone. I looked down, fiddling with my bookbag's zipper, but not before he'd caught me staring.

"You like?" He smiled slyly, holding out the charm, an *O* with a line through the center. I'd seen it before.

"It's Greek, right?"

He nodded. "Do you know the letter?"

I shook my head. "My grandmother knew the language but never taught me."

"It's theta." He was looking at me expectantly.

"Mmm. Very nice." Him, the charm, all of it.

He smiled and let it drop back to his chest. "Which way?" Zander asked.

I gave him directions, canvassing the car as we drove. Beyond the classic rock station, there was little evidence of Zander's personal tastes. His car was as generic as Jackson Kennit's apartment had been.

"Who do you live with?" he asked. Most people assumed I lived with parents but of course I'd already told Zander I'd lived with my grandmother in Pennsylvania. Past tense.

"A friend. Her name's Petra. She works at a mental hospital," I added, shifting to see his reaction. "The one where I thought I saw you."

Zander's expression stayed completely neutral. "Ah. So that's why you hang out at the nuthouse."

"Sort of. But I was really there visiting Demetria."

He said nothing.

"Do you know her? Demetria Kansokis? I thought you might, since she probably goes to *your* church."

He shrugged, eyes still totally focused on the road. "Maybe she does. Like I said, I don't go all the time. And I certainly don't know everyone there."

"You seem pretty *in* with the Greek community, though," I

persisted. "All the people you hang with at school, your church . . ."
I really didn't have anything else.

We had turned onto my street and Zander guided the car into
an empty spot by the front of our building. He turned to me, the car
still idling.

"You seem very interested in the Greek community," he
observed.

"Yeah, I guess." I scratched at a smudge on my jeans, hoping I
didn't sound stalkerish and trying to come up with a version of
the truth confessional enough that he'd believe it. "I'm probably
way off-base thinking this, but I'm kind of short on family and it
seems like being Greek—in the community and all—makes you
part of something. Gives you a connection I guess I'd like to have."
I glanced up, giving him a half smile that felt sadder than I'd
meant it to. "Pathetic, huh?"

Zander smiled back, his eyes almost kind. He was silent for a
minute, then said, "Why don't you come to my house for dinner
this weekend?"

I couldn't possibly have heard that right. "What?"

"My mom's a great cook. You know, like your typical Greek."
He was teasing me now, but gently. "She'd love it if I brought a
nice Greek girl like you home."

"But . . ." I was totally floored. He wanted me to meet his
mother? Have dinner with his family? "You hardly know me,
Zander," I said hesitantly, not wanting to offend him and not at all
sure what his invitation meant.

"So I'll wait a little longer before I propose."

My obvious and total confusion made him laugh.

"Really, Cassie," he said. "Lighten up. You seem like a nice
person—a little lost, maybe, but nice. If you're so interested in us

Greeks, come on over and study us in our natural habitat. No pressure."

"Uh . . ." I smiled weakly, feeling like a kid who'd spun herself dizzy. "Yeah, I guess." I recovered my manners enough to add, "Thanks, Zander. That's really nice."

We settled the details. Saturday night. He'd pick me up.

I was getting out of the car, my head still whirling, when Zander leaned across, catching my wrist gently in his strong hand. "And just so there's no mistake," he said, his near-black eyes fixed on mine, "I *do* like you."

I don't even remember him letting me go. I stood on the sidewalk watching him drive away, that smug smile still on his lips. My heart was pounding and I felt hot enough to give off steam in the frigid Illinois winter. What was I getting into?

chapter 15

At the wake on Saturday, Mr. Ludwig had to ask me three times to replenish supplies in the ladies' room.

"What's wrong with you?" Ryan asked after Mr. Ludwig had gone.

"I don't know. Nothing," I mumbled, feeling bad about disappointing Mr. Ludwig, who was clearly annoyed. But that couldn't begin to compete with the other stuff I was feeling. Nervous, excited, and nauseated at the thought of tonight. Meeting the family of the boy I was finally willing to admit I had a huge crush on, though I barely knew him.

I couldn't figure out Zander Dasios at all. He wasn't the bad boy with a heart of gold, but he also wasn't just the bad boy. He was, as Liv said, smokin' hot, kind of a jerk, and definitely high on himself.

But there was more to him. Even Jack had never held a door for me. And who invites a near stranger to his house for dinner because she's lonely? Well, and because he liked me, an idea that would have made me squeal if I were at all the squealing type.

I spent most of the day avoiding Ryan, who kept wanting to talk about religion. It wasn't that I wasn't interested, but if I couldn't focus enough to bring toilet paper to the bathroom, how on earth could I discuss Hinduism versus Shintoism?

Finally, the interminable wake ended, the last of the teary mourners went out the door with me right on their heels.

I ran home, waving at Petra when I passed her at the building entrance.

"Good luck on your date!" she called, jogging toward the El.

"It's not a date!" I yelled back.

"Right!"

Liv had had the same reaction. Of course, she and Erin accosted me even before first bell the day after Zander drove me home. I played it off the best I could, but I couldn't keep the giddiness off my face, I guess.

"Honestly, Cassie," Liv had said, hands on her hips and look-ing imperiously down at me from her Scandinavian tallness, "you expect us to believe he's inviting you to dinner at his house—to meet his family—because he feels bad for you? You don't really think that, do you?"

I didn't know what I thought. But I definitely found it hard to imagine that Zander Dasios invited every girl he liked to meet his mom before he'd even gone out with her. So I tried not to believe anything. Or think anything. Or feel anything. All of which was, of course, completely impossible.

Zander was right on time, escorting me to his beat-up car with the same tongue-in-cheek gallantry as the last time.

He had a classical station on, which made me smile because I'd never have expected it, yet it totally fit. It reminded me of Nan and thinking of her helped settle my nerves. A little. Enough that I could carry on a conversation with Zander, something that in the half hour before he got there, I'd begun to doubt.

But he was surprisingly easy to talk to, his superiority and arrogance softened in our aloneness.

"I'm an only child," he told me as we drove through back roads, dark except for his headlights, though it was barely seven o'clock. "No brothers or sisters and totally spoiled because of it. As you might imagine."

"I've probably seen more spoiled," I said, thinking of Erin's huge house and Ryan's brand-new car.

Zander smiled. His long fingers tapped the wheel, alternating as if he were playing along with the piece on the radio. "Do you play piano?" I asked.

"I do. Since I was five. You?"

I shook my head. "But my grandmother loved classical music. I've heard this one a gazillion times."

"Yeah?" he said. "I forget what it is."

"Haydn. Sonata No. 62."

"Wow." He glanced over, then nodded. "Yeah. My mom's going to love you."

Zander's mother was stunning, as elegant as her son was hot. And gracious and totally devoted to him. I'd been picturing dark hair piled high, overdone makeup, overeaten baklava—God knows why, since Nan, the only Greek mother I'd known, was nothing like that.

His father was nowhere to be seen. Every photo in the house was of just the two of them, which I guess kind of summed it up: he wasn't in the picture. I thought of Nick Altos's family, his mom also a single parent, but I was pretty sure this was a different story. Calliope Dasios seemed about the last person who'd ever get caught up with a druggie ex-con.

"Zander tells me you're new to the area," Calliope said, passing a basket of rolls across the mahogany table. She'd insisted I call her by her first name.

"I am. I moved here about three months ago."

"From Pennsylvania."

"That's right," I said, feeling a tingle inside. Zander had been talking to his mother about me. Not just my name, but details.

"And you're on your own, more or less?"

"Well, I live with a friend, but yeah . . . I mean, yes," I corrected, matching Calliope's precise diction. "I don't have family here."

She nodded, motioning Zander to refill our water. As he reached for the crystal pitcher, I took another look around the dining room. The furniture was heavy carved wood and the walls were filled with paintings in gilt frames and shelves of "antiquities," as Nan's friend Agnes called them: ornate boxes, odd-looking tools, a bronze and glass candelabra. It looked expensive and a little overdone. Like the Greek church.

"Your parents are no longer living?" Calliope asked, interrupting my thoughts.

"They died when I was two." I decided to leave it at that. Much simpler than the whole truth.

I glanced at Zander, who'd been mostly silent since we got here. He was watching us with a thoughtful and slightly unfocused expression, but smiled when he caught my eye.

"So why did you come to Bellevue?" his mom was asking.

"Well . . ." I hadn't really had to explain that to anyone. People didn't ask once they found out my parents and grandmother were dead. That usually stopped them cold.

"Why not?" Zander joined in finally, saving me. "Who wouldn't want to live here? I mean, why go to Florida—or Greece, for that matter—when you could move to the windy city with the coldest winters this side of Minnesota?"

"Yeah," I said, grinning. "I didn't really consider the weather before I moved. What about you?" I asked Calliope. "Have you always lived here?"

"No," she answered. "We moved around quite a bit when Zander was younger. Since he's been in school, I've tried to stay put. It isn't always easy." Calliope's dark eyes twinkled. "I'm afraid I'm a bit of a vagabond by nature. I like to see different places. Collect." She gestured toward the walls and nooks of the room. "You may have noticed."

I smiled too. Calliope had a way about her that made me feel uniquely comfortable, as if she were taking me into her confidence and sharing secrets. "I did notice," I said. "So you . . . collected . . . all of this traveling?"

She nodded. "It's what I do. I've turned my bad habits into a living. I'm a dealer of antiquities and ephemera. Mostly for high-end designers and the occasional private client. But some of the things I've found"—she glanced around the room again—"I just couldn't part with."

Dinner was delicious—chicken with feta and olives, salad, fresh bread.

"I went with something simple," Calliope said, almost apologetically. "Zander asked me to give you a real Greek experience, but he wasn't sure what you liked. Next time we'll know better." She smiled, but I was stuck on *next time.* As in, I'll be coming here again. With Zander. He'd barely joined in the dinner conversation and I was afraid to look at him—what if *he* didn't want me to come back? But when I glanced over, he winked and my pulse raced.

Calliope served dessert and I told her about my summer in Kansas with my aunt; she told me about the inlaid bowl she'd gotten from a dig in Tunisia. Zander still said almost nothing. A strange and unsettling idea—subtle but insidious—crept in that maybe he hadn't really *wanted* me here, but *needed* me. As cover. *My mom would love it if I brought a nice Greek girl like you home.* Is that what I was? A stand-in date to keep his mother happy? Calliope was clearly attached to her son and not afraid to confront. Not stupid either. If even a fraction of the rumors about Zander were true, she had to know. I could definitely see her interrogating Zander more than he cared for.

I was glad when it was time to say good night. Talking to Calliope had been interesting, but grew less so the more I thought about Zander's detachment. I stood by the car while he spoke to his mom for an extra minute, wondering how to ask why he'd brought me here without sounding totally insecure.

I didn't have to.

I heard the front door close and turned to find him there, right behind me. So close that I could see faint stubble on the soft olive skin of his jaw. Wordlessly, he leaned forward, bracing his arms on the roof of the car, pinning me in, and kissed me.

My head spun, the word "swoon" coming to mind. A helplessly outdated word that was exactly how I felt. There was no connection between thought and feeling, just a crazy, light-headed, weak-limbed dizziness that left me breathless even when he stepped back, a tentative half smile on those full lips that had just been on mine.

We didn't speak. I couldn't take my eyes off him, feeling

something I'd never quite felt before. Something not me. Attraction almost beyond my control.

Had it been this way with Lucas and Jack and I'd forgotten? I didn't think so. There was something too penetrating about Zander, the way he looked at me too deep. And I was helpless to cover myself, my feelings embarrassingly naked.

I looked down, saw my hands trembling slightly.

He leaned close and for a heart-stopping second I couldn't breathe, sure he was going to kiss me again, but he reached past, pulling firmly on the car handle, the door bumping me lightly on the butt.

"Get in," he said softly.

In the silence of the car, in the seconds before he joined me, I tried to slow my heartbeat. I had no idea what to say to him.

He slid into the driver's side, started up the car, air blasting from the vents on high, where we'd left it when we parked. Zander lowered it to a soft whisper and rubbed his hands together before looking over expectantly, still with the slight smile.

"I have no idea what to say to you," I told him.

His smile deepened. I saw a twinkle in his dark eyes. "Tell me how you feel."

I looked down, mumbling, "I think that's obvious."

"I want to hear it."

Of course you do. His arrogance was less charming when I was so obviously being toyed with. "I feel confused, Zander," I said, my voice steadier than I'd expected. "You taunt me at the mall and school, then invite me to meet your mother but completely check out of the conversation. Then you come out here and kiss me like . . ." I stopped for a second, caught up in the dizzying memory of it.

"Like we're lovers?"

My face turned bright pink—who on earth says "lovers"? "Like we're more than strangers," I said deliberately.

"It's almost as if I like you or something, huh?"

I refused to play along. "Normal people don't act like that, Zander."

"I'm not normal."

"No shit."

He sighed, backed the car out, and started to drive.

I stared out the window in stony silence, unwilling to budge until he did. The last thing I needed was some mind-gaming pseudo-boyfriend. Still, my heart froze at the idea of telling him to eff-off.

We drove the five or so miles to my apartment in silence, large and awkward despite the classical music that played and the weight-less drift of flurries brushing gently across the windows.

Zander pulled up in front of my building and I reached for the door handle, ready to spring out without even a thank-you, my infuriation having grown to a live and pulsing thing.

"Cassie . . ."

I paused, hand still on the door, face averted.

"Look at me, please."

I did. Gritting my teeth.

"Listen." His voice was soft. Cajoling. "I know I didn't handle tonight very well." He looked down hesitantly and I tried to ignore my cynical side calling him out for the calculated move. "The truth is, I really do like you and it's been a while since I've actually said that to anyone."

I scoffed. "Zander, you don't even know me."

He met my eyes. "You don't know me either and you like me, don't you?"

I didn't answer and he didn't make me.

"Sometimes," he said, "attraction is just that. A gut feeling that builds into something more. I know enough about you, Cassie, to see the 'more' that could be there. Maybe I shouldn't have brought you home. That was probably a mistake, having you meet my mom before we knew each other better. But you had a good time, didn't you?"

"Yeah," I said grudgingly.

"And maybe I should have butted into the conversation more, but you and my mom seemed to be hitting it off. I thought you liked talking to her."

"I did," I said, starting to feel like a jerk.

"And I definitely shouldn't have kissed you like that," he said, flashing his devilish smile. "But I just couldn't help it."

I looked down, smiling too.

"If I promise to be a gentleman, can we go out again? Somewhere normal, you know, a movie or something? I promise not to try anything funny, like holding your hand or . . ."

I held up my palm. "Okay, stop." I smiled at him. "I'm not trying to make a big deal of this, Zander, but you just threw me, especially after the things . . ."

I stopped, not wanting to admit the gossip, but he was a step ahead. ". . . that people say about me?"

I shrugged.

"You think I don't know people call me a player? Please, Cassie," Zander said, rolling his eyes. He turned serious then, looking searchingly at me. "They're right, you know," he added. "But not this time. I'm not playing you. I promise."

It was enough to make my heart stop. And definitely to make my brain stop, because who believes a player when he says something like that?

Me. That's who.

chapter 16

I drifted around the apartment like I was in a dream the rest of the weekend. Liv called and texted, dying for scoop, but I didn't want to shatter the euphoria of remembering Zander's eyes on mine, that kiss, the things he'd said. Speaking them aloud would and I couldn't *not* talk about it. Liv would never let me. So I put the phone on mute and left it on my dresser. Though I strolled casually by every half hour or so, just to see if Zander'd tried to reach me.

He'd sent one text early in the day, a "thanks for last night." Even his words typed on the screen were thrilling, as if they'd been whispered in my ear. Liv was right. I had it bad. It made me smile to admit it.

"Not a date, huh?" Petra said from her chair by the window as she caught me grinning foolishly for about the fiftieth time.

"Okay, maybe a date," I answered.

"Tell!"

I did. And Petra said he sounded delicious, which of course he was.

* * *

I was nervous walking to school on Monday. I hadn't heard from Zander the rest of the weekend. Not a big deal. He said he wanted to hang out again, but it wasn't like we were exclusive. Or even anything, really.

I hoped I could pretend that's how I actually felt.

He wasn't at his locker when I passed and I wondered whether he might be waiting at mine, but when I rounded the corner, I saw only Erin, Liv, and Hannah, ready to pounce.

"How was it?"

"What happened?"

"What's his house like?"

"Does he have any brothers?"

I laughed, holding up my hands. "Easy, guys. Stop." The sharp edge of nerves relaxed. "Hannah, it was great," I said. "Liv, I had dinner with him and his mother, then he drove me home. Erin, his house is nice." I paused, thinking about the dining room, filled with old things. "Unusual. His mom collects stuff. Antiques."

"Did he kiss you?" Liv's eyes gleamed.

"That would be awfully forward, wouldn't it?" I said innocently. "I mean it was only dinner . . ."

"Cassie!" Liv practically stomped her foot. "Did he?"

"Yes," I answered, forcing myself to sound blasé.

"Aha! I knew it!" She lowered her voice. "Was it amazing?"

"Um, yeah." I turned to my locker, fiddling with the lock to get a grip on my emotions, which were flying so high it seemed equally possible that I could laugh hysterically or burst out crying.

"Oh, Cassie, that's so awesome! I've got goose bumps for you," Liv said, adding, "But still . . ."

I glanced up. "What?"

"Just, you know, be careful."

"Because he's a player?"

"Well, yeah."

"Yeah, I know, Liv. We talked about that."

"You did?"

"Uh-huh." I traded the books in my bag for those of my first- and second-period classes and swung the door shut. I turned to face the three of them, all leaning forward like they might pull the words from my mouth. "He said he knew that's what people said about him and they were right. But that he's not playing me."

It sounded defensive, even to my ears.

"But," Hannah jumped in, rescuing me from Liv's skeptical look. "You never answered my other question. Does he have a brother?"

Everyone laughed and we started down the hall, Liv changing the subject—thankfully—to her first weekend as a working girl at TREND.

He found me at lunch.

I'd dreaded going in there, afraid he'd be sitting at his usual table with his usual friends and ignore me, as usual, proving Liv right. But he didn't. I'd just paid and was walking with my tray when he spoke, his voice close behind, making my back shiver as if he'd touched me.

"I've been looking for you."

I turned, my tray sticking awkwardly between us. "Hey, Zander." It came out cool. Perfect. Much calmer than I felt.

"Let me take that." He reached for the tray, carrying it easily to the side with one hand so he could walk close to me. Close enough that I could see heads turning as we passed. "I thought I might see you at church yesterday."

"I had to work."

"Oh, so you got to see your boyfriend then."

I was confused for a minute. "Ryan?" I looked up to see him smirking.

"So that's his name."

I played along. "Mm-hmm. Yeah, we spent the day together. It was very romantic, side by side over a dead body."

Zander paused. "What?"

Oops. I'd been working so hard on my banter that I'd totally forgotten to pay attention to what I was telling him. Too clever for my own good. "Yeah," I said, still walking, forcing him to keep up. "I guess I forgot to mention it. I work at a funeral home."

I was cringing inside, wondering if he'd just veer off, back to his table without another word, maybe even taking my lunch with him in his hurry to escape.

"That's weird," was all he said. We'd gotten to my table, Liv, Erin, and Hannah already sitting there, trying desperately not to look up. Zander put my tray down. "Hi, ladies," he said smoothly.

"Hey," they all answered.

He turned back to me. "I'll leave you to your lunch, but are you free on Friday?"

"I have to work."

"Graveyard shift?"

"Ha-ha. No, but I probably won't be done until around ten."

"Okay, I'll pick you up."

"Sure," I said, even though it hadn't been a question.

"Great." He smiled, his teeth sparkling white against bronze skin. "We'll talk details later. Just tell Ryan you're spoken for."

He walked away, true to his word to be a gentleman. He hadn't tried to touch me or hold my hand, much less kiss me again.

Be careful what you wish for, I thought.

chapter 17

I'd meant to go to Vauxhall Hospital after school on Monday, long overdue for a visit to Demetria. Instead, I went home and cruised the social sites for Zander. Nothing. I wasn't surprised. There was something more sophisticated about him and his friends—who I still didn't know and who continued to ignore me in the halls—to think they'd be chatting online. Whispered confidences and smoky nights out seemed more their speed.

I thought about going to see Demetria on Tuesday instead, but Hannah asked me to do something. She and I had never hung out alone before and I didn't want to say no. We ended up at TREND, where Liv convinced me to buy an outrageously expensive sweater for my date with Zander.

"He will not be able to resist you in that," she said when I stepped out of the dressing room. I wouldn't have given it a second glance—pale blue, hip length, fitting soft and snug over my few curves. It looked both innocent and touchable.

Liv's manager rang me up—raving about Liv the whole time—then Hannah and I went next door for yogurt. It turned out we didn't have much in common other than our friendship with Liv—she didn't read much, I didn't know the actors she talked about, and we had no classes together. I thought later that it was probably only seeing me with Zander that'd made her invite me out. She was far from the only girl at school with a crush on him.

He'd texted me about plans for Friday and sent a few other quick messages—"thinking of you" and "how's your day, beautiful?" Cheesy stuff that still made me tingly inside. But we hadn't done more than wave, smile, and say hey in the hallways and lunchroom at school.

I probably would have drifted through the whole week that way, mindlessly counting down the hours until Zander picked me up, if I hadn't run into Nick Altos.

I'd stayed at school late to finish up a science project and was bundled up and headed out the door when I saw him sitting on the bottom step of the deserted staircase, his head in his hands.

"Nick?"

He looked up, startled. My chest squeezed when I saw his tear-stained face. Guilty, guilty, guilty.

"Hey," I said sympathetically, walking over to him.

He sniffled. "You have a knack for finding me like this."

I sat carefully and waited. When he didn't speak, I prompted gently, "Want to talk about it?"

Nick shrugged jerkily, almost convulsive. "What's there to talk about? It's the same shit. My dad." He paused, breathing deeply for control. "At first it sucked because . . . well, it just sucked. He was dead. I wasn't going to see him again. That was bad, but it wasn't so . . ." He stopped, his mouth quivering, and looked at his hands. "So personal."

I kept my eyes averted. After a minute he continued, his voice harder, strained. "I went to his apartment. Just me. My mom didn't want to go. I don't blame her and I'm glad she wasn't there. It would have just been harder . . ."

I thought of the picture next to the bed, knew already what Nick had found. The same kind of stuff I'd found cleaning out our apartment after Nan died. Photos, cards, years of memories that had meant enough to keep.

". . . Father's Day," Nick was saying, his hands balled into fists. "Pictures of me dressed like him for Halloween. The letters he wrote were the worst. Four of them, stacked inside a drawer. All for me. All unsent." Nick's next words were partly strangled by emotion. "Telling me how sorry he was. How he was going to be better. You know that dad in commercials?" His voice rose, a little hysterical, but I let him go on, trying my best to squelch the guilt that kept rising like bile in my throat. "The throw-the-football-let's-go-fishing guy? The one I never had? He wanted to be that guy," he said, his hands still clenched, their knobby knuckle ridges white. "And now he never will."

I didn't reach for him or do anything but sit there quietly while he got it together. When he was calmer, I tried to reassure him, feeling like the biggest fraud in the world the whole time. He nodded, seeming embarrassed, and I thought: who the hell am I to comfort the kid whose dad I let die?

I went to see Demetria that afternoon.

chapter 18

She trudged in, looking sloppy and disheveled, her belly rounder than I remembered, though it had to be my imagination. It hadn't been *that* long since I saw her and it was way too early for her to be showing.

Sitting there, looking at Demetria and remembering the awful conversation with Nick, I couldn't believe I'd let so many days go by without coming. What was I thinking, allowing my golden opportunity to tick away, minute by minute, like this? It made me angry with myself and determined to get it out there today, even if I had to ask her point-blank. Demetria would be released someday, maybe soon. I'd wasted so much time already.

I leaned in close, smelling the industrial clean of generic detergents wafting from her gown. "Demetria," I said, speaking low, to be sure the nurse behind me wouldn't hear. "I need to talk to you about your visions."

It took a minute, but slowly her eyes drifted up, connecting with mine. I felt a surge of elation.

"There's a reason I've been coming to see you so often," I said urgently. "It's not just because I needed someone to talk to. That was true, but really it's that . . ." I paused, her eyes watching me as if through a steam-fogged mirror. Medicated? I didn't know what they could give a pregnant girl, but she didn't look all there. I willed myself to go slowly, though everything in me wanted to spill it all out. "I think you and I have the same"—don't say problem—"ability."

There was a flicker, a light breeze of recognition that stirred Demetria's placid features. I leaned closer, my hands almost touching hers. She didn't flinch.

"My mom could do it too," I said. "I didn't know her, but I'm sure of it. She was in a place just like this and I read her files. When she told them about it, they thought she was delusional."

Demetria's eyes were clearer, still focused on me. Though she hadn't spoken yet, I could almost feel it coming. We were on the verge.

And suddenly, I realized that this might be it: the moment I would know the truth about whether there were others, whether I truly was descended from the Fates, born with something beyond ability. Responsibility. Learn whether there was a consequence to my actions beyond what I could see or imagine. Whether each life I saved truly sacrificed another.

I squeezed my hands together and took a deep breath.

"I'm hoping you can help me understand it, Demetria, what we can do with the mark—"

"Don't."

I looked up, startled by the voice interrupting me, familiar and out of place. He stood just behind me, close enough to touch.

"Zander?"

He stepped around the chair to face me and shook his head, saying it again. "Don't."

"Don't what?" The words came out automatically, without

conscious thought, my brain too busy trying to fit together the disjointed pieces before me:

Zander, where he'd denied ever being.

Looming over me and this girl I'd counted on as the key to my past and future.

The word he'd spoken.

Don't.

My anxiety was different from a minute earlier when I'd been on the edge of telling Demetria my secret. This was a throat-closing dread.

"Don't tell her," he said.

A chill went through me. My words were weak and totally unconvincing. "Tell her what?"

Zander didn't bother answering, just held out his hand. "Come with me."

I stood numbly, my brain frozen. Firmly, he grasped my arm above the elbow, pulling me to the door. I could feel the heat of his touch through my sweater. Zander led me past the nurse, who glanced up, nodded, and checked off my name as I exited the room.

I was dizzy. Not in the warm, exciting way I usually felt around Zander, whose face was tight and determined. This was a disoriented, upside-down dizzy. I let him pull me along, not sure I could command my feet unguided. Not sure I had much choice anyway. We passed hallways and doors, down elevators and through waiting rooms. I shrugged on my coat just before the final gauntlet of sliding magnetic exits that ushered us outside, the Midwest winter like a slap in the face.

Zander gently pushed me against the brick of the hospital wall, glancing quickly to either side, before leaning in close exactly as he had less than a week before when he'd kissed me, pinned against his car.

"What were you thinking?" he hissed, his breath hot and angry in my ear.

I couldn't answer, fear and confusion choking my words like an invisible collar.

"Yes, Cassie," he said, pushing back. Crossing his arms. "I know what you are." Zander smiled, but his eyes weren't warm. They were hot. Burning into mine. "You knew there were others, didn't you?"

I was mute. My mind still grasping, fumbling. Understanding, but trying not to.

"Of course you did," Zander said, hitting the heel of his hand against his head as if he'd just made the connection. "That's what you've been doing here, visiting Demetria. Every week, right? Sometimes more." He shook his head again, chiding now. "Where did you ever get the idea she was like us?"

Us.

Of course. Why hadn't I considered it before? And then I realized why.

"But you're not a girl."

Zander frowned with mock disappointment. "You just figured that out? I'd have thought with the kiss and all . . ."

"That's not what I mean. I thought . . ." I stopped, still not sure it was safe to say it out loud. Did he really know? How could I believe him? Of course, I'd been ready to believe in Demetria, who'd given me no reason to think she was anything other than a troubled pregnant teenager.

"Let me help you out," he suggested wryly. "You thought the Fates were women."

"Yes."

"And their power only went to female descendants."

"Right."

"I'm not a descendant of the Moriae," he said, fingering the gold charm hanging from its black leather cord. "The theta," he instructed. "I thought when you were staring at it in my car, you knew. And when I realized you didn't, I could see how clueless you were about all of it."

"So you're not a Fate," I said, struggling to follow along.

"Right."

"Then who—what—are you?"

"I'm a descendant of Thanatos, half brother to the Fates. I claim the soul."

It sounded absurd, but the jokes that normally would've sprung to mind wilted. He was still fingering his necklace, deadly serious. And looking at his face, I knew it was true. All of it.

There *were* others and I'd found one. Not Demetria—Zander.

It was a sickening feeling. Especially when what he'd said made its way through the frazzled circuits of my brain.

"You . . . you kill them?" I whispered, barely able to say it aloud.

Zander rolled his eyes. "No, I don't kill them, Cassie. I'm a soul guide. I expedite."

"You expedite," I echoed stupidly. "What does that mean?"

He didn't answer. We stood there silently for a minute, me still leaning against the wall and Zander standing tall and powerful before me. Light was fading from the sky, a deep purple gray that threatened snow or rain. Drips of water had frozen midstream from the lip of the downspout beside me. I was too numb to feel it, though, colder inside than out.

"We should go somewhere more private," Zander finally said, his eyes looking deeply into mine.

My pulse sped up, as if it still thought Zander was trying to get me alone so we could kiss rather than talk about death and our roles in it.

I followed him mutely to his car, thinking back to the first time he'd driven me home after school. I'd felt giddy—happy and nervous all together and even a little scared, but in a good way—about riding with this boy Liv and my own better sense warned me away from. *He's dangerous*, she'd said.

She didn't know the half of it.

Zander drove to his house.

"Is your mom home?"

He shook his head. "She's in the city. Working. It wouldn't matter, though," he added. "She knows about you."

Of course, I thought dully. He still hadn't explained how *he'd* known about me, but I figured I could just add that to my massive list of questions.

Inside, the faintest scent of incense and Greek tea hung in the air. It was a sudden, aching reminder of Nan, so unexpected and bittersweet that my eyes filled with tears. I tried to wipe them away, but Zander saw.

"Hey . . ." He stepped closer, his hand brushing my cheek lightly. Zander pulled me close, which made it worse because I felt that crazy attraction, but it was all mixed up now. He wasn't who I thought he was. I hadn't wanted him to be who I thought he was when I thought he was a player, but I didn't want him to be this either.

Or did I? Would it be better having a partner with benefits or just more confusing?

I was having trouble thinking straight and there was so much to think about. I shook my head and pulled away, turning my back to discreetly erase the remaining tears. "Thanks," I said hoarsely. "I'm fine."

"You're new to this." Zander sighed, almost to himself. "I have to remember that, try to be more . . . sensitive."

It wasn't a word that suited him. "It's okay," I said. I'd stopped crying, but my eyes and nose were probably still that awful shiny red. I sat on the sofa, looking down so Zander couldn't see the ugly mess I'm sure I was. He took the armchair next to me.

"I guess I have a lot of questions to ask you," I said finally.

He nodded. "I thought you might."

"Can you tell me what you know?" I said without looking up.

"Why don't we start with what *you* know," Zander suggested. "I'll fill in the blanks."

I nodded. "Okay." And then had no idea what to say. I decided to start with what I'd been about to tell Demetria when Zander turned my world inside out. "I know that I see something," I said. "The mark, I've always called it. It's like a glow around someone and it means they're going to die."

I raised my eyes, almost afraid to see what he thought.

"Mm-hmm," Zander prompted casually, like we were talking about a test at school or a movie we'd both seen. "So you know the moment they're going to die?"

"Not exactly," I answered. "The light is on them all through the day of their death, as far as I can tell."

His expression flickered, like the shutter on an old camera, a momentary change of emotion I couldn't quite place. And then he said, "Anything else?"

I looked back down. It was easier to say it that way. "I know that I can change things. I can tell them what I see, what I know, and they live."

"Sometimes," he corrected. "Right?"

"Right," I said, remembering the ones who died anyway. "Sometimes."

He nodded.

"I know ...," I started, pausing when I realized there really wasn't a single other thing that I knew. Not for sure. "I guess that's all I really know."

Zander disagreed. "You knew there were others."

"Well, yeah. There was a letter in Nan's things, written in Greek. She gave it to me when I turned sixteen, but I never bothered with it until after she was gone and I realized that the mark was more than just knowing about death. It was an ability to delay it."

"And the letter said ... ?"

"It said I was a descendant of Lachesis, one of the three Fates of Greek mythology."

"Responsible for determining the length of a human life," he finished.

"Yes."

"That's it?" Zander asked.

"No," I said, looking up to catch every nuance of his reaction. "It said I could change the course of fate, but only at the cost of another life." I felt everything in me tense as I asked the critical question: "Is it true?"

He nodded. Without hesitation. "Yes."

"How do you know?"

"My mom told me."

"But how does *she* know?"

He shrugged. "She just does."

"Has she ever seen it happen?"

Zander looked confused. "Seen what happen?"

But she wouldn't. That wasn't her gift. It was mine. I could picture how it would look, the mark disappearing from one person and reappearing on another. Someone in the same scene, unmarked before.

What was the likelihood I'd ever be there to see it? The mark wasn't like a fly, moving through physical space, or a germ, passing from one person to another. I'd never know who'd been sacrificed. Never know if anyone truly had been. I'd have to take it on faith. Or not. Kind of like religion, which is what it had been for the ancient Greeks. But I was a seventeen-year-old high school student, not a Greek goddess.

Maybe the original Fates were just girls like me, too. Normal people. Maybe they all were—Jesus, Buddha, Allah, Krishna—none of them gods at all, but regular people with bizarre, extraordinary abilities or really good tricks; Jesus's walking on water nothing more than finding a sandbar underneath.

It was the chicken and the egg. Untestable. Unprovable. You either believed or you didn't.

Diagonally from me, Zander sat, waiting expectantly for whatever else I had to say.

"That's it, I guess," I told him finally. "That's all I know."

He nodded, but said nothing.

"So?" I prompted finally.

"So, what? Are you asking me what I think?"

"No. I'm asking you if it's true. Me—us—being some kind of descendants of Greek . . . gods."

"Yes," he said, annoyed at having to answer it again. "Of course it is."

Of course. Right. How could I have thought otherwise?

"What about you?" I asked.

"I'm a soul guide."

"So you said. But what is that exactly? Do you know when someone's going to die?"

"Yes."

"But you don't cause their death?"

"Right."

"But you also don't do anything about it."

Zander frowned. "No, I do what I'm meant to. I expedite, help the soul get to where it belongs."

"Like a fast lane to hell?"

"Or heaven. Whatever they've earned in their life. But yes." He nodded. "That's not far off."

"So, you're like . . . saving them the afterlife paperwork?"

"That's a very earthly view."

"It's the only one I have, Zander."

"Right." He sighed and ran a hand through his loose curls. "Try to think broadly, Cassie. Metaphysically. There's more to the workings of the world than you can frame in our terms."

"So explain it to me."

"A soul guide's role . . . ," he started, but seeing my expression, stopped and shook his head. "I don't think you're ready to listen."

"What do you mean? I'm listening."

"No. You're sitting there, frowning, with your arms crossed," he said pointedly. I looked down. He was right: classic defensive posture.

"I'm sorry, Zander. You're right," I said, wondering why I wasn't feeling the way I thought I would if I ever found out there were others. I was feeling sad. Disappointed. Not that I'd found someone—but that it was Zander. "I think you just caught me off guard with this whole thing," I told him, my heart aching a little as I said it. "I thought there might be others like me out there. I just didn't expect it to be you."

"What? You weren't waiting this whole time for me to tell you I was the angel of death?" He wasn't grinning, but I could tell he was holding it back.

"No," I said, smiling weakly. "That was a bit of a surprise."

Then I realized what he'd said, the way he'd described himself: angel of death. It's what Demetria had called her visions. Had I been right about her all along?

"Wait . . . is she one too?" I asked, confused.

"Who?"

"Demetria."

"We've already been through this," Zander said shortly. "No. She is not."

"But she knew about you, didn't she? She told her mother she'd had visions, seen the angel of death."

Zander looked down, picking uncomfortably at the frayed knee of his jeans. "Sometimes they can see. Just a little bit. I don't know exactly how." He shook his head. "It's happened to me once before. Both times they were Greeks. Maybe they had a touch of the blood, distant relatives or something."

"Huh." My brain was sluggish, unable to come up with anything more intelligent. It hit me then that I was exhausted. Completely drained. How could I not be after going from Nick to Demetria to Zander to this, the truth I'd been seeking?

Outside the sky was black. Like despair, my overwrought mind offered.

"I've gotta go," I said to Zander.

"Okay," he said. "We should talk more, though. There's a lot to cover . . ."

"Another day. Please. I can't take any more right now. Really."

He drove me home. I watched dim shapes pass by—road signs, houses, cars—their images moved across my brain like Rorschach inkblots, meaningless and forgettable.

We pulled up in front of my building and made plans to meet again, talk more. As I was reaching for the handle, Zander said, "I was wondering . . . all these weeks you kept trying to get me to admit I'd been at the hospital with Demetria. Why?"

"I thought you were the father of her baby," I said simply, feeling silly to be reminded of my oh-so-human crush, the worries I'd had about Zander. Stupid nothings compared to the truth.

"She's pregnant?"

I nodded. "When I saw you there, or thought I saw you, I . . ." I shook my head, embarrassed.

Zander snorted. "I can see why you were worried about me. First your friend tells you I'm a player, then that." He smiled. "It's a wonder you ever went out with me at all."

"Yeah." I smiled too, surprised to find it still a relief to have him confirm there was nothing between them. He hadn't even known she was pregnant.

Then he said, "You understand now why I was hanging around her."

No. I hadn't. But suddenly I did—her bandaged wrists, the reason she was at the hospital.

The warmth of our shared moment turned icy.

"Were you with her when . . . ?" I couldn't even say it.

"No." Zander didn't elaborate and I didn't have the strength to ask more; I wasn't even sure what the questions should be.

He leaned over to kiss me before I got out, but I didn't have the heart for it. Thinking about him lurking, waiting to be a part of her death put a serious damper on romance. I turned my head and it became nothing more than a chaste and brotherly peck on the cheek.

chapter 19

Back in Kansas, when I learned that my mom hadn't died the way I thought she had, I had to wait for the library to open to find out more. Drea, my aunt, only had a laptop that she shuttled from work to home to the airport and back again. I guess I could have looked for an Internet café or something, but that hadn't occurred to me at the time. When your world is rocked, you don't always think straight.

Like now.

I sat in the quiet of our apartment, wishing Petra were home so I'd have an excuse to avoid the computer that sat patiently in front of me.

But she wasn't. Reluctantly I lifted my eyes to the screen, where my news-filled homepage glared brightly. A message scrolled across, offering pain relief, then listing about a hundred side effects you could expect if you took it.

Out of the frying pan, into the fire. I knew all about that.

I typed in the name. It seemed to expand ominously as the letters built one upon the next: THANATOS.

I'd heard it before, of course. Maybe from Nan, in the bedtime stories she used to tell. Definitely in my earlier research. I'd spent hours online and at bookstores and libraries after reading the translated letter that claimed I was a descendant of the Fates. But there was surprisingly little to learn about them, and far more fiction than fact. The Fates made it to TV and video games and books, but though Christianity has the Bible and Islam has the Koran, Ancient Greece has nothing. Maybe their sacred texts were destroyed when the religion was outlawed, leaving only myths about myths.

What sources existed were full of errors, calling the Fates immortal and ugly, a trio of weavers and spinners. None of it applied as far as I could tell. We were definitely mortal, I didn't *think* I was ugly, and I'd earned solid Bs in Home Ec, only for effort, not skill with a needle or thread. My pillows and wash bags came out lumpy and crooked without fail.

The things I'd read made me doubt the letter and its claims more than believe them. Maybe that's what I'd wanted. Now I was back at it, trying to pick truths from these flawed sources, not about my ancestors this time, but about Zander's.

The first thing I learned was that the articles called him Death.

He said he didn't kill them. Most of what I read claimed otherwise.

But I did find a few sites that talked about Thanatos as a guide—what Zander asserted he was—leading souls from one world to the next. The Ancient Greeks thought most people went to Hades, which, despite being cold, damp, and dark with the dead bumbling around like pathetic ghosts, was *not* the equivalent of hell. That was Tartarus, for the very wicked. Elysium was their heaven. Without proper death rituals, the soul would struggle to gain access to its proper realm, suffer during the passage, or be trapped indefinitely between worlds. This, according to Zander and two of the thirty-plus things I read, was where Thanatos came in.

I'd been so caught up in the tornado of revelations about myself that I'd learned almost nothing about Zander's role—what exactly he did and how. Online it said Thanatos and his brother, Hypnos, carried off the dead or enveloped them in a black cloud. I couldn't imagine Zander walking around suburban Chicago with dead bodies or surrounding them with a spooky mist and getting away with it.

I was about to give up, my vision blurry from reading the convoluted language of ancient writings that seemed to be taking me nowhere, when a quote from Thanatos in a two-thousand-year-old play by Euripides caught my eye: "The woman goes with me to Hades's house. I go to take her now, and dedicate her with my sword, for all whose hair is cut in consecration by this blade's edge are devoted to the gods below."

I printed it out, remembering how the first day I'd spoken to Zander, he'd held my hair, twisting a lock of it between his fingers. *Beautiful*, he'd said. *Don't ever cut it.* It gave me chills. Was that how he did it?

It was easy to imagine a consecrated blade—a sword, a knife, even an old pair of scissors—among all the antiques in his house.

I sat back, trying to assimilate what I'd read, what I'd heard from Zander, and what I'd known before. What was true? What did I believe?

I believed there had once been Fates and that I was descended from them, even though I still had no real proof. Only that Zander had known what I was, things about me that I hadn't told him. And then there were the notes in my mother's file. And the letter and the myths Nan had told me throughout my childhood that, in retrospect, seemed more purposeful than just bedtime entertainment. All of that taken together was like person after person telling me the sky was red. Like the people in the Greek Orthodox church, I now believed.

The question remained: what was I supposed to do about it?

chapter 20

Zander and I met by his car, parked in its usual spot outside school. It was Monday, five days after he'd hijacked my visit with Demetria. He'd pushed me to get together sooner, talk more. Even texted me over the weekend, but I'd said no to everything. I needed time to think.

I'd picked up hours at Wilton & Ludwig instead, wearing scrubs Friday night while my new "date sweater" stayed home. Ryan and his dad were loading up stuff for the annual Funeral Directors Convention in Milwaukee. They'd be gone this weekend, Ryan told me, but maybe we could try a synagogue next week? Maybe, I agreed vaguely, our visit to Zander's church feeling like a hundred years ago, though it had been less than two weeks.

At school, I'd sensed Zander watching me. By my locker, walking to class, leaving homeroom. I pretended he wasn't there, but in truth, I felt him more than ever, as if there were an invisible string connecting us. Binding us.

"Zander's staring at you," Liv told me at our table in the cafeteria.

"Yeah."

"Well, why doesn't he come over? You have a fight?"

"No, not really. We're just taking a few days." I shrugged. "Like a cooling off period, you know?"

She glanced over my shoulder, where I felt Zander's eyes searing into me. "He doesn't look cooled off," she said, raising an eyebrow. "He looks like he wants to eat you for lunch."

I didn't feel cooler either. As days passed, things just got more jumbled. I wished I could forget that I'd wanted to be *with* Zander and approach him with a rational game plan like I'd had before coming to Bellevue. But I couldn't do it. I felt an overpowering need to see him, so now, standing near his car, every inch of me was zinging with anxiety and anticipation.

My stomach flipped as he walked out of the school's doors, the wind making him wince slightly. He came toward me, wearing the same intense look I had pictured in the lunchroom. The one I'd seen when I glanced sidelong down the hallway toward his locker each day since we'd last spoken, always finding his eyes on me, as I knew I would.

He stopped just inches away. We weren't touching, but the space between us was so charged that I knew even if my eyes had been closed, I'd have felt him there. He paused for the shortest second and without waiting for a hello or any sort of consent, reached down, sliding a hand behind my neck, into my hair, his bare skin somehow hot against mine despite the rawness outside, and kissed me so forcefully that I lost my footing, bumping into his car.

"I've been waiting days to do that," he whispered, holding me steady as he pulled away.

I looked down at my boot kicking leftover snow so he couldn't see the things I knew he would if I met his eyes. My head was buzzing. I felt him slip his arm around me, the only thing keeping me upright as he guided me into the passenger seat.

I studied the fuzzy gray ceiling while Zander rounded the back of the car, recalling the things I'd read about Thanatos. Get a grip, I told myself. This is not just a hot guy from school. This is Death, or some version of him. Nothing is surer to have an unhappy ending than swooning over Death.

I heard the rush of wind, a swish and rustle of fabric as he sat, the double-click latch of the door closing firmly. Then silence. For a minute, neither of us spoke. It was still freezing in the car and I squeezed my gloved hands together, the leather crinkling and stretching.

"Zander . . ."

"I know," he interrupted, his voice low and earnest. "I promised I wouldn't do that again. Truly, I couldn't help it."

I rolled my head to the side and found him watching me, smiling, but without any irony or mischief. As if he was sure I'd understand what he meant. I did.

I took a deep breath. "We need to stay focused," I said primly, as much to myself as to him. "There's a lot I don't understand and I need to."

He nodded briefly, then faced forward, shifting the car into drive. "I know."

Zander pulled away from the curb. Out the window, I watched bundled students hurrying home. We passed Hannah and Erin and I waved quickly. I'd face twenty questions in the morning, if not sooner.

Before I came face-to-face—and closer—with Zander by his car, I had planned for this to be *my* conversation. I told him everything I knew last time. He gave little besides confirmation.

Today, I'd find out the stuff *I* needed to know. But it hadn't exactly started like I'd expected.

"I've been doing some reading," I told him as we left school behind.

Zander nodded.

"They call Thanatos 'Death.'"

He shrugged, eyes on the road, cucumber cool. "Yes."

"But you don't kill them?"

"I already told you I don't."

I let out my breath, unaware I'd been holding it in the seconds it took him to answer. He *had* told me before, but it was a relief to hear it again. "You're a soul guide."

"Right."

"How do you do it?" I asked, rubbing my lips gently. The bruised feeling of his kiss had faded, making it easier to concentrate. "What exactly do you do?"

"I take the necessary actions to escort the soul to its proper realm."

It sounded like he was reading from a textbook. "C'mon, Zander," I scoffed. "You can do better than that."

"No," he said, glancing at me sharply. "I can't."

"Well, do you need to be with them?"

"Yes." He leaned forward, checking street signs, then turned left.

"So you need to be at the deathbed of all these people?"

"Not exactly," he said evasively, "but I need to be with them. At some point."

"Don't the police get suspicious? I mean, isn't that like a telltale sign of a serial killer or something? Someone who's always showing up at crime scenes or around people who wind up dead?"

"I've been questioned once or twice."

"Really?"

Zander shrugged. "It's not a big deal. I didn't kill them. It's not like it's ever the same cop. This is a big city, Cassie. Not some one-traffic-light burg."

Yeah. That's exactly why I'd come here.

"So what happens if you're not there? With people about to die?"

"What happens if *you're* not?" We'd stopped at another red light, Zander glancing out his window, then mine, before settling his eyes on me.

"I guess things just play out the way they would have any-way," I said slowly, adding, "In which case, maybe it would be better if I was never there."

"Talk like that'll get you tossed in the lock-up with your buddy Demetria," Zander warned with a smile.

"I didn't mean like that, Zander." I wasn't going to let him drag me off-track. "So if you're not around, the person doesn't get escorted to . . . Hades?"

He laughed outright. "Hades? You know no one calls it that anymore, right? That went out, um, about two thousand years ago."

I flushed. "No," I said crossly, glad the green light forced him to look away. "I guess they forgot to put that in my descendant-of-the-gods training manual. Along with everything else."

"Listen," he said, squinting at a street sign, "I think you're get-ting too wrapped up in worrying about stuff you don't need to. The important thing is that you've got this ability for a reason. You have a role, a job to do. Don't worry about my role—it doesn't con-cern you."

"Actually it does," I said. "It concerns me a lot. I am very concerned."

"What are you so concerned about?"

"I'm concerned that you know people are going to die and can ignore it so easily. Don't you feel like you should try to help them? Maybe not all of them, but there must have been some, somewhere along the line, that you felt like you should have warned."

"No. There haven't been. It's not my job to warn them."

"That's like the guards at Dachau saying it wasn't their job to help the inmates. Just following orders. Is that what you do, Zander?"

"I'm not a bad guy, Cassie. You of all people should understand that."

"Yeah. Right," I said. "After all, you're saving them lots of time with the post-death paperwork and everyone knows when you're dead, time is money."

Zander pursed his lips. "You're not taking this seriously."

"Zander, I assure you, I couldn't take it *more* seriously."

"Then why are you being flip?"

"I'm not being flip. Or if I am, it's only to try to show you how ridiculous what you're saying is. How come, if we both know someone's going to die, it's up to me to decide whether they should or not, but you have no responsibility?"

He started to answer, but I cut him off. "Yeah, I know, Zander, because it's my role, not yours, right?"

"Yeah, Cassie, that's right."

"Even assuming for a minute that's true, which I'm not saying it is," I said, "how could I possibly know who to save and who not to?"

"You just know."

"But, Zander," I said, feeling the sudden sting of tears. "That's the problem. I don't."

He frowned, glancing over, then right back to the road. I tried to explain.

"I'll give you a perfect example," I said. "I was in town with Liv one day and saw this old guy sitting out in the cold, with the mark. Everything about him told me I shouldn't warn him. I mean, what good could it possibly do? The guy wasn't going to suddenly cure cancer or save the world from nuclear war or even be there for some sad kid trying to grow up, like Nick Altos."

Zander looked confused and I realized I'd never even told him about *that* mess.

"I warned him anyway, the old guy. And you know what he said?"

"What?"

"So be it. I'm ready."

Zander shook his head. "You should have known better."

"I did," I said. "But when I got out there, I couldn't *not* do it. And then I felt so bad about making that mistake and putting someone else's life on the line, that I went too far the other way and let Nick Altos's dad die for no reason."

Zander raised his eyebrows.

"Yeah, I was there. I didn't know who he was, but I saw the mark, I followed him. Spent a whole day doing my damnedest to learn enough about him to make a good decision. And in spite of all that, I couldn't even find out he was the father of one of my classmates, who's a good guy and totally crushed by it."

"So what's your point?" Zander asked quietly.

"My point is . . ." I stopped, wanting to be sure I said it exactly right so maybe he could give me the answer, help me figure out how to live. "My point is I don't know how to decide. More than that, I don't know if I can. I'm not sure if I can live with the idea that what I do—or don't do—leads to someone else's death. I've tried to believe it's their actions, their choice, that everything they do leads up to the moment where I see them with the mark . . ."

"That's what you should believe, Cassie."

I shook my head, thinking of how I'd told off Lucas at the end of philosophy class in Kansas. *People are responsible for their own actions*, I'd said. *In making choices, they accept the outcome.* I'd tried so hard to believe it, to live it. "The truth is, Zander, I think it's impossible for me to walk away from death like that. I don't know how you can, role or not. You still know they're going to die. But worse for me is the idea that if I *do* intervene, I'm damning someone else." I shook my head at the frustration of the ultimate catch-22.

"You're too human," is what Zander said. "I'm going to help you get past that."

That's what we'd come to.

Zander was driving more slowly now, his head tilted slightly as if he were listening or watching for something. I looked out the window, trying to find a restaurant or shop or coffeehouse or any likely destination, but metal gates were pulled down over the storefronts and the people hurrying down the streets didn't look like they'd be friends of his. Nothing about the neighborhood suggested it was somewhere we would visit. Or *should* visit.

"Where are we going, anyway?" I finally asked him.

Zander pulled to the curb and shut off the car, answering with a single word. "Hunting."

chapter 21

We stood on the sidewalk, between Zander's car and the store-fronts lined with garbage bins. I still had a hand on the car's roof like it was home in a game of kick the can. Somewhere safe.

"What does that mean?" I asked.

"It means exactly what you think," Zander said, reaching for my hand. "Let's go."

I crossed my arms, leaning back, fully against the car now. It took him a few seconds to realize I wasn't coming. Zander dropped his outstretched hand.

"What?"

"You don't really think I'm just going to follow along, do you?"

"Listen." He exhaled, a short, frustrated sound. "You want to know how this works? Then come with me."

"I get it, Zander. The mark means they're going to die, so I decide if it's the right time, you do your . . . whatever." Because of course, I still didn't know what he did—his *necessary actions*. It gave me the shivers and I shook my head. "I'm not sure I want to do this."

"I don't get you at all," he said. "On the drive, you were dying to know. Here I am now, ready to *show* you, and you won't let go of the damn car. What's the deal?"

"I *do* want to know. I'm just not sure I want to actually be, like, a part of it. Right now. Here." I glanced around at the dirty streets, pulling my coat a little tighter.

"Well, we don't really have much of a choice, do we, Cassie? That's the bitch about death, you don't get to pick the time." He smirked. "Well, actually, *you* do, but you know what I mean."

We stared at each other for a minute. A stalemate.

"Look," he said, when it became obvious I wasn't moving. "You have to come along. I need your help."

"With what?"

Zander jangled his car keys, looking down the dim, near-empty street, before answering. "I don't know who it is," he said finally. "Or if it's the right time. My gift is meant to be paired with others' gifts, just like yours. That's how they used to work." He spun the keys impatiently, flipping them around a finger, then back again: *tah-ting, tah-ting.* "I've learned how to do it on my own so that I can usually find them, but getting the timing right is much harder."

"What if you don't?" I asked, then backtracked, realizing I had never considered that his gift might be different from mine in this way. "How *do* you find them, anyway? What do you see?"

He shook his head, dark waves swaying slowly. "I don't see. I feel." Zander's eyes narrowed, his vision turning inward to cull the right description. "It's like . . . I sense their weakness, their muscles moving slower or their heart struggling, as if the body knows it's almost done, like it's giving up. Even the young ones. When they're near, I smell decay, though nothing's in the air." He shook his head at the insufficiency of words. "I don't know. It's like a combination of smell and sight and hearing at a very essential and primal level."

"Like a predator seeking out his prey?"

Zander made a face, not amused.

"So, you feel something, but . . . ?"

"But it doesn't always mean it's the right time. I learned that pretty early on," he said wryly. "My mom's tried to help, but she doesn't have the gift."

"She doesn't?" I'd suspected as much, but wanted to hear what he'd say.

"No. Mine passes only to the males in the line, just like yours passes to the females."

"So your father . . . ?"

"Had it."

I asked it more directly. "Where is he?"

"Gone." It was like watching a padlock snap shut on Zander's lips. There'd be no more discussion about *that*. It was too cold to stand out here wasting time, so I went back to my earlier question instead.

"So what happens if you get it wrong?"

"I'm not sure," Zander admitted. "I've been told that doing it too late forces the soul to wander indefinitely and being too early steals a part of their essence. In real life, sometimes it seems like nothing happens. And sometimes they get"—his face darkened, something forbidding passing across it—"fucked up."

I shivered, imagining the memory of what he'd done. "Has that happened a lot?" I asked.

"Not a *lot* . . ."

But way more than it should. "Maybe you shouldn't be messing around with your gift, if you're leaving people fucked up."

"And maybe you shouldn't be trying to save people when you

have no idea how or who you're sending to their death in doing so," he countered angrily.

Touché. We glared at each other.

"Anyway," he said crossly, "you can solve the problem by telling me when it's the right time."

I shook my head. "I really can't help you, Zander. I don't know anything beyond the day."

"That," he said deliberately, "is exactly what I need to know."

"Oh." It clicked neatly into place. Of course. I was his perfect match. The yin to his yang.

"Now you see why I need you," Zander said, stepping closer and looking into my eyes so intimately it was as if we touched. "We belong together."

His voice had the huskiness of deep emotion and I was so drawn to it—to him—that I barely noticed I'd let him slip his gloved hand in mine until he tugged it gently, whispering, "Let's go." Slowly, he took a step, then two backward, his gaze unwavering.

Dazed, I felt myself peeling away from the car to follow him down the cracked sidewalk, shadowed in the colors of dusk. We walked, hand in hand past corrugated metal barriers shielding the closed stores, doors with buzzer boxes for the apartments overhead, and a convenience store, the only sign of life, with racks of newspapers, magazines, and candy squeezed into its tiny space. At the corner, we waited for cars to pass. There was a bar there, the kind with an anonymous door and windows high on the wall, like those in Jackson Kennit's basement apartment.

"Where *are* we?" I asked Zander.

"Nervous?" He smiled and tucked his arm protectively over mine, pulling me closer, our gloved fingers still intertwined.

"No," I lied, ignoring the tingly feel of being beside him. "Just curious. I've never been here."

"I imagine not," Zander said, nudging me to start across the now-empty street. "This is Norwood. Not one of the city's best areas. Not one of the worst either."

We walked halfway down the next block in silence. I had the same feeling I'd had driving here. That Zander both knew and didn't know where he was going.

"Are you, like, following a trail or something?"

"Yes. But someone seems to have eaten all my bread crumbs."

"For real, Zander. Can you feel that there's one here?"

"Yes. I've felt it for days. I've been trying to pinpoint who, but figuring out that it's here is as close as I've gotten." He frowned. "That's why I've been trying to get you to come with me, but you were oh so cooperative. We're lucky it's not too late."

"Why didn't you just *tell* me?"

He stopped, looked at me directly. "Would that have made a difference?"

"Well . . . uh . . ." I fumbled, not sure of the answer myself. If he'd told me at school that he needed my help to do his bizarre "duty," would I have come?

"Right," he said, reading my doubt. He started walking again and I felt his grip tighten, holding my hand firmly, as if to be sure I didn't escape. "That's what I thought."

He moved fast and I had to trot every third step or so to keep up. "So you're waiting for me to see the mark?"

"Well, unless someone jumps out and screams 'I'm dying,' yes."

"But I thought you could find them on your own."

"Usually I can," he said evenly. "But I've been walking around down here for days, so clearly I could use some help with this one."

I thought about that as we moved briskly down the windy

sidewalks. If I didn't tell him, there's a chance Zander would never find the person. Then what? They were going to die whether we were there or not. At least if we found them, there'd be a chance to do the right thing. Whatever that was.

"Don't you think we should try looking in some of the buildings or something?" I asked. "There's no one out—"

And then I saw her. Saw *it*, to be exact: the glow of the mark, partially hidden behind a Dumpster.

I stopped short, stumbling as Zander jerked my arm, not realizing I was no longer moving.

He turned and saw me staring down the alley. "Ahhh." The satisfaction in his voice was clear. "You found him."

I didn't answer. Slowly, I walked down the narrow passageway. Zander had let go of my hand but was close on my heels. It must have been something about the way her legs were positioned, maybe the size of the feet I'd seen protruding that made me sure, even at first glance, it was a woman. She was sleeping, clearly homeless, with tattered, dirty bags full of unidentifiable stuff surrounding her like the walls of a fortress. Her own private empire of trash, like the "Shopping Bag Lady," a story I'd read as a kid. It always made me sad, even though at the end she opens up a store and sells her "treasures." This lady wouldn't open a store, maybe never even open her eyes again.

Behind me, I felt Zander moving. From the corner of my vision I could see his hand in a coat pocket, poised for . . . something. I whirled to face him.

"What are you doing?"

He raised his eyebrows. "My duty, Cassie. That's what we're here for. To help him."

"It's not a him." It pissed me off that Zander was ready to send this lady's soul off and couldn't even get her gender right.

He leaned forward, peering around the Dumpster. "Oh. Right you are." He shrugged. "Fine. I'm going to help *her.*"

I took a step to the left, blocking his path. "Don't you think we should talk about this first?"

"Talk about what?" Zander looked genuinely confused. "You see the mark, don't you?"

I nodded. "Yeah. But . . ."

Understanding, then incredulity, washed over his face. "You're not really thinking of trying to *save* her, are you?"

"I just think . . ." I trailed off, not really sure what I thought or what kind of argument might hold water with Zander or whether I should even be making an argument.

He took a deep breath then, more gently than I'd have expected, said, "Come here." He took my hand again and led me nearer to the woman, filthy blankets wrapped around her. "Look at her, Cassie."

"Yeah, I know—"

"No," he interrupted. "Really *look* at her." He squatted down so that, had she opened her eyes, she'd probably have been literally scared to death by him sitting so close. "What do you think she has to live for?" he asked softly.

My eyes traveled over her pale face, gray stringy hair matted on the side where she leaned against the frozen Dumpster. She sat on an old cardboard box stained with grease, her body bloated and covered by shapeless, colorless clothes. The answer brought tears to my eyes. "Nothing," I said hoarsely.

Zander nodded slowly, his eyes never leaving mine. "Would you really trade someone else's life for hers? So she could sit here longer? Spend another night wondering if she'll freeze to death? Another day thinking about—"

"Stop," I whispered.

Mercifully, he did. Silence hung between us, everything suspended. But I didn't know what to do. What I *should* do.

"I'm going to do my job now," Zander said quietly. "Her time could be any minute—any *second*. This is the best thing we can do for this woman, Cassie—give her soul peace."

He watched me for a moment more, waiting. I might have nodded or Zander might have taken my silence as consent. I don't exactly remember, too swallowed up in the rush of sadness and guilt and horror at how this could be: her, him, me. He bent forward, the dim glint of metal shone briefly, reflecting the glow of the mark around her. And then darkness.

The mark didn't fade like a sunset blending into night. It vanished, like a bare bulb clicking off. But the impression of the glow remained scorched into my vision. She'd been alive. Now she wasn't.

I'd let that happen.

And then Zander was beside me, turning me away from where I knew she was, though I could no longer see her clearly without the mark.

"Cassie," he murmured, words washing over me as he led us down the alley, away from what we'd done. "It was her time. If it hadn't been her, it would have been someone else. Have you ever seen someone more ready, more *deserving* of death?"

I didn't answer. How could I? Zander was so confident, without a trace of arrogance, just a quiet certainty that he'd done the right thing.

I couldn't imagine ever feeling that way.

chapter 22

He drove me to school the next day. I wouldn't have gone otherwise, was in pajamas when he showed up, ringing the buzzer at six thirty.

"What the fuck?" I heard Petra mumble, shuffling to the intercom. She is *not* a morning person.

She stuck her head in a minute later. "It's your boyfriend. He's on his way up."

I thought about asking why she'd let him in, but that's the thing about having a roommate instead of a parent. Monitoring my social life isn't her job. "'Kay," I said. "Thanks."

She waited a few seconds, then asked, "Aren't you going to get up?"

"Wasn't planning on it."

"No offense, Cass, but I thought you liked this guy and you look kinda like . . ."

"Like I just woke up?"

"Well, yeah."

I shrugged, still lying on the bed. "If he doesn't like it, he can go to Hades." She didn't get the joke, of course. It wasn't funny anyway.

A minute later, I heard the soft knock, their voices, then Zander at my door. "Good morning, sunshine."

I rolled over, hugging my pillow and squinting up at him. For a second, I wished I'd taken Petra's advice. Zander was watching me with an amused smile, his skin radiant in the morning sun.

"What are you doing here?" I asked.

"Making sure you're okay." He came over, sitting carefully on the edge of my bed, tilting his head, eyes searching my face. I couldn't stop my heart from racing. It was like a chemical reaction, the smell of him making me light-headed every time.

I don't think I said a single word to Zander the whole drive back the night before. I know he was talking, but his words made no sense, drifting past as I watched lights outside the car window, trying to forget where we'd just been.

I wondered how long it had taken the police to find her. That's the one thing I did remember clearly: waiting for Zander's car to pull away and then stumbling back outside, walking block after block until I found a pay phone—they *do* still exist, I wasn't sure—not wanting to use anything that might be traceable. I'd quickly given them what I knew, the Norwood cross streets I fixated on while walking dumbly to his car. Then I hurried back to the apartment. For the shortest second, I'd thought about texting Jack. It occurred to me that it had been days—no, weeks—since I'd been in touch, so wrapped up in Zander. Thinking about Jack pained me in a different and deeper way now, one I didn't want to consider at all, colored with shame and regret and an abyss of longing for the normalness of what we'd been, something that seemed beyond recovery. I'd taken Nyquil and went to bed instead.

"I'm okay," I told Zander now.

He reached over, slowly running his fingers over my face, into my hair, pushing the strands back lightly, his touch both tender and seductive. He leaned down, kissed my cheek, then my forehead, before whispering low against my ear, "Then get up."

I felt short of breath, the numbness of the night before gone, my whole body tingling and taut and *wanting* as he lingered there.

Zander leaned back, studying me and smiling in a way that told me he knew exactly what I was feeling. "I'll wait in the car," he said. "Don't be a slowpoke."

I tried but wasn't that successful. My body followed simple commands—get up, shower—but my brain was sluggish, probably using all available circuits to block out memories of the woman in the alley. I stood, still dripping and towel wrapped, in front of my closet, the hurdle of choosing clothes completely insurmountable.

"Cass?" Petra paused outside my door. "You okay?"

I smiled weakly. "Yeah. Just tired, I guess."

Petra took a step closer, leaning against the frame. "Late night last night," she observed.

"Yeah."

"Guess he couldn't stay away, huh? Had to come back first thing this morning?"

"Right."

Petra raised an eyebrow, asking more directly, "Is everything okay with you and . . ." She waved a hand toward the door.

"Zander."

"Right. You and Zander. You're not . . . in any kind of trouble, are you?"

Oh, I thought, I'm definitely in trouble. Much worse than Demetria's kind of trouble. See—Zander and I—we killed a woman last night. She was going to die anyway, but so am I and so are you. Doesn't mean we did the right thing by not saving her. I'm in horrible, sickening, un-sort-outable trouble, thanks for asking.

"No," I finally answered. "I'm not in trouble."

Petra raised an eyebrow, not buying it at all. She waited a few seconds before saying, "You know, Cassie, I might not be your mom or dad or grandma, but I *am* your friend. And a shrink to boot. I'm good at keeping secrets and pretty decent at helping people. If you don't want to tell me, that's totally cool, but if you need an ear—or a hand, a lift, a few bucks, anything—I'm here."

I nodded, letting my hair fall forward to shield my face. I was on way-too-thin emotional ice not to cry. "Thanks," I said hoarsely.

She stepped into the room, letting me pretend I wasn't a weepy mess, and said, "I'm not much of a fashion consultant, but since you don't seem to be making much progress here . . ."

And that's how I wound up dressed in an orange skirt, combat boots, and plaid shirt, knocking on Zander's car window forty minutes later.

"That's an . . . interesting look for you," he said as I slid into the seat.

"Petra picked it out."

"Yeah." He pulled away from the curb. "It's, um, fierce?"

I didn't answer.

He let music—classic rock today, Clapton or Cream—fill the silence until we were about halfway there. Then he launched into what he'd come for. "You know we did the right thing last night, Cassie."

I said nothing. He'd expected that, plowing right ahead. "I *know* you know it. In your heart. Maybe it'll take a day or so for the shock to wear off, but you know it'd be hard to find someone more ready to die. I know you know that too. But I want you to *feel* it."

Zander turned down the block, letting guitar riffs fill the car until we pulled into a spot outside school. He turned the key, shutting off the engine and the music, and faced me. I looked away.

"What we do is hard, Cassie," he said earnestly. "But it's *right*. And it's easier when you have a partner. Someone who can help you and support you. Especially when it's someone who cares about you."

I met his eyes, looking for the truth, because this was part of Zander I couldn't figure out at all. Did he care? Or was it just attraction? Or the need to pair up with someone who could see the mark?

"Yes, Cassie," he whispered, as if reading my mind. "I do."

His eyes held mine, dark and deep and vulnerable, asking me to accept him. To believe.

This is what I wanted, what I longed for. Someone to share the mark with. It was like I'd been squashing myself down into a tiny hole, barely able to breathe with the effort of holding in this horrible secret, and Zander had come along and, without a second thought, offered a hand to help me out. A strong, sure hand that would stay in mine, making sure I didn't get lost.

"Do you think that woman's in a better place now?"

"I'm sure of it," Zander said without a moment's hesitation. "We helped her get there, Cassie. *And* made sure the wrong person—someone less ready—didn't go in her place."

He opened my door for me, as usual, and I took his hand, letting him lead me out of the car and into school.

* * *

"You'll never guess what I got in the mail yesterday," Liv sang when she caught up to me after calc.

On three hours of nightmarish sleep? And after a pop quiz that I could barely read, much less answer? You're right, I won't. "What?" I asked.

She held up a booklet, practically jumping up and down. I squinted at it. *Tonleigh College.* I raised my eyebrows. "For you?"

"Yup," she said proudly. "They have fashion merchandising in their business program. It's what my manager majored in and"— Liv paused dramatically—"she thinks I might even win one of TREND's scholarships."

"Wow. That's awesome, Liv." I tried really hard to sound enthusiastic, but it came out dull and hollow. Exactly the way I felt. I hoped she'd be too keyed up to notice, but she stopped, looking hard at me.

"You okay?"

"Yeah," I said, continuing down the hall. "Bad sleep last night."

Liv kept up. "Did something happen with Zander?"

"No."

"Are you sure?"

"I'm sure," I said. Because when I got right down to it, it wasn't Zander's fault. He had nothing to do with me or him being what we were. It just was. "Why do you ask like that?"

"I know you won't want to hear it," she said, "and I don't have anything against him, Cass. Really. I mean, he is unbelievably hot and if you're happy with him, I am. But the thing is, you don't seem that happy."

"I don't?" I asked tiredly, completely proving her point.

"No. You seem a lot less happy, actually."

There wasn't much use trying to convince her otherwise so I told her a semi-truth. "It's just coincidence, Liv. I *have* been feeling a little down, but it isn't Zander. I think it's just that I'm kind of . . . homesick."

"Really?" She looked at me sympathetically.

"Yeah. I mean, it's great here and I've met you and Zander, but it's not quite home to me yet. And I miss . . . well, lots of stuff there."

"Hey." Liv put her arm around me, giving a squeeze. "I'm sorry, Cass. You're so chill I forget how tough things must be for you."

"Thanks, Liv," I said shakily. "And congrats on the college thing. I really am psyched for you."

"If I decide to apply," she said breezily. "Just food for thought." She stepped away, giving my Petra-picked outfit a once-over. "So are you okay or do I have to wait till tomorrow to rag on you for wearing orange? And, uh, the rest of that ensemble?"

I smiled. "Rag away."

chapter 23

I half expected an article about a dark-street homicide, but when I finally found her obituary, it was an in-column write-up like any other. It was two days after her death and, having read and discarded the obits from each prior day, I'd started to wonder if the police had written me off as a crank caller. I imagined her still sitting, undiscovered, in that alley. But a mention of the West Norwood Women's Shelter caught my eye. Her age fit. Lucy Edwards was her name. She'd died of pneumonia. It sounded so normal.

I barely noticed Ryan entering the break room, completely absorbed in the paper. The mental image of how we'd found the woman—the alley, the horrible condition of her clothes and belongings—was still so vivid, I guess I'd been looking for that description in her death notice. But of course it wouldn't be there. They don't tell you that someone died a terrible, lonely death, filthy and surrounded by squalor.

"What's wrong?" Ryan said, sliding into the chair across from mine.

I glanced up, frowning. "Nothing. Why?"

He raised an eyebrow. "You're staring at the obits and looking like your best friend died." He paused. "She didn't, did she?"

"Of course not." I looked back at the paper. "It's just this woman . . ." I wanted to talk about it even though I knew Ryan was the wrong person. Zander was probably the best choice, though I wasn't sure he'd really understand either.

"What about her?" He leaned forward, taking hold of the page to turn it so he could read. "This one? Lucy Edwards?"

I nodded and let him take the paper from me, figuring out what I wanted to say—what I *could* say—while he read.

He handed it back to me, shrugging. "What about her?"

"It just seemed weird to me," I said slowly, "how she had all this history, this normal life. A job at a bank, a family—daughters, grandkids." Things I never would have expected that sorry, rag-wrapped woman in the alley to have had. "And yet her last residence was a homeless shelter."

Ryan looked confused. "So?"

"I don't know," I said. "I just wonder how it came to that. Why didn't she wind up a happy grandmother, reading or playing with little kids or something instead of dying in a dirty, frozen alley?"

"Did it say that?" Ryan reached for the paper.

Shit. "No." I pulled the paper away, waving my other hand dismissively. "It's just an example. You know what I mean: how does someone with all the stuff of a normal life end up in a home-less shelter? Why didn't her family help her?"

"Maybe she was on drugs. Or was an alcoholic," he said. "Happens more than you'd think."

"Yeah, maybe."

"If you're so curious, go to the wake," he said, smiling a little. "Spy on the relatives. That's your thing anyway, right?"

"Ha-ha."

"You could do it right out in the open," Ryan said. "See who shows, what they're like. Tell them you were . . ." He thought for a minute, then finished triumphantly, "A volunteer at the shelter!"

It wasn't a bad idea. I'd never been to the actual service of someone I'd seen with the mark. Never felt like I'd be able to handle it. This was the one to go to, though. A test to be sure that what Zander and I had done was really, truly right.

"Listen"—he leaned in conspiratorially—"I'll even go with you. We'll say we were both volunteers come to pay our respects."

"Oh no, you don't have to do that, Ryan." But it was too late, he was already swept up in the idea.

"I don't mind," he said. "Really."

Maybe it'd be better to have him along. He might do the talking, letting me concentrate on who was there and what kind of woman Lucy Edwards had been, what had happened to bring her to where I'd found her. And, most important, whether redemption might have been possible if I'd given her another chance.

"Okay," I told him.

We got there just after five thirty, the start of visiting hours.

"Ready?" he asked as we parked in the lot across from the funeral home's heavy wooden door.

I shook my head, feeling nauseated. I'd seen plenty of dead people and plenty of people with the mark. But I'd never seen a before and after.

"Come on," he said, nudging my arm gently and smiling. "Don't tell me you're nervous? Not the Cassie Renfield who tiptoes around the funeral parlor, catlike, spying on unsuspecting mourners. I don't believe it."

"I guess I wouldn't make much of a secret agent, would I?"

"Terrible," Ryan agreed, getting out of the car.

I followed him to the front door, both of us walking quickly in the dark winter night. The truth is I was beyond nervous. About talking to her relatives and seeing her, but mostly that I might learn that Zander and I had made the wrong decision.

He'd thought I was ridiculous when I told him about the obituary. "Of course she had family," he'd said. "What do you think— homeless people's mothers and fathers and siblings just evaporate when things go south for them? Life is a series of decisions, Cassie. Somewhere along the line, this woman made one—or a bunch— that sent her life in the wrong direction. The other people in her family didn't. It's not hard to understand and it certainly doesn't change the fact that her life was over. Done. Physically, emotionally, potentially."

I could tell he was getting tired of reassuring me. But it *did* help. I always felt better in the face of his certainty.

The entry hall of the funeral home—one of the nicest in the city, according to Ryan—had polished wood floors covered with a dark Persian carpet. A brass chandelier glowed overhead. I scanned the mourners as we waited for our coat-check slips. There were about thirty people milling around, surprisingly well dressed in conservative suits and skirts, like any of the visitors I'd seen at Ludwig & Wilton. I tried to pick out the family members, but none resembled the slumped and slovenly woman I'd seen in the alley.

Until we passed the portrait. It was an oil painting, two girls and a boy in their early twenties, a dog, a fireplace. The girls looked so similar they might have been twins. Next to the painting were two smaller photographs. One was a group shot, a bride and groom in the center. The other was the three siblings again, in a similar pose, perhaps thirty years later. I stared at it, hardly able to believe that the dark-haired woman smiling tentatively at the camera was actually Lucy Edwards.

"I guess one of them is her," Ryan said. He nodded toward the chapel entry just ahead and to the right. "Should we find out which one? Pay our respects?"

I wasn't sure I could. My throat felt too tight and I desperately wished I hadn't come. This was everything I'd hoped not to see. Family. A history that wasn't squalor and abuse and poverty, but the kind of upbringing that should have led to . . . well, anything but where it had.

"Cassie?" Ryan, who had taken a few steps toward the doorway, turned and looked at me, his eyebrows raised. "Are you coming?"

I nodded mutely. My feet felt encased in cinder blocks, but I forced them forward. One, then the other, until I was beside him.

He frowned, whispering, "You okay?"

I nodded again, forcing another step. *Clomp.* I could see into the room now: wooden chairs scattered throughout, wall sconces dimmed, groups of people talking in hushed voices, glancing now and then toward the front of the room. And the casket. Just the foot edge of it. Dark wood, gleaming like the surface of a frozen pond. It stopped me cold.

Ryan stepped closer, gently touching my arm. I looked up at him, standing beside me with real concern in his eyes. It was a tenderness that was hauntingly, achingly familiar and I realized three things simultaneously:

One, Ryan liked me. *Really* liked me. In a way I should have—and probably had—recognized a long time ago, though I hadn't wanted to admit it.

Two, I felt things for him, too—except they weren't for *him.* They were for the honest and caring part of him that reminded me so much of Jack, who always made me feel like things would be okay, even when they might not be. Something I desperately, *desperately* needed now.

And three, Ryan wasn't Jack.

I took a deep breath and smiled weakly. "Sorry," I whispered. "Felt a little dizzy. Maybe something I ate."

"Do you want to sit?" Ryan glanced toward the small sofas lining the wall. "We could—"

"No, no. That's okay." I smiled again, but it felt more like a grimace. "Let's just go in."

"Okay." Ryan took my hand and gave it a little squeeze. It might have been comforting if I didn't feel so bad about who'd *really* been on my mind each time I was with Ryan. Still, I let him lead me into the chapel and to the casket.

We stood silently facing Lucy Edwards. I didn't recognize the woman laid out before us any more than I'd recognized her in the photos and painting out front. She looked like a slightly older version of any one of my friends' mothers. Lightly wrinkled with tasteful makeup and brown-gray hair neatly framing her face.

It struck me that there was every possibility this *wasn't* the woman Zander and I had seen. All I'd been going on was her age and the fact that she'd spent some time at a shelter in the same neighborhood where we'd found the woman with the mark. Nothing concrete, really. This whole excursion could very well be a colossal waste of time. The woman from the alley wasn't someone who had a family like this that might have helped her, cared about her, reconnected with her, had they known. She was nothing like that at all.

I nudged Ryan. "You ready?" I wanted to go. Quickly.

He glanced down at me. "Not feeling good?"

I shrugged, noncommittal. I was feeling fine. Just ready to be away from this scene—the dead woman, her family, Ryan-who-wasn't-Jack. All of it.

He nodded, still grasping my hand as we started toward the foyer.

I recognized Lucy Edwards's sister near the exit and almost headed for the opposite door, but Ryan saw her too, automatically steering us that way to offer the required condolences before leaving. If there's one thing you learn working at a funeral home, it's the importance of etiquette.

"You're Ms. Edwards's sister?" he asked when the guest before us moved on.

"I am. Julia Redmond," she said, her voice thready, her smile forced but kind.

"We knew your sister from the shelter," Ryan said smoothly. "She was a lovely person. I'm so sorry for your loss."

"My condolences, as well," I added formally, thankful for Ryan's years of practice and my months of eavesdropping.

Julia Redmond looked like she'd been punched.

In a moment of perfect clarity, I knew there was no use pretending this was a mistaken identity and unfortunate waste of time. Lucy Edwards *was* the woman from the alley.

Her sister's mouth opened and closed once, then twice, fish-like, before she spoke. "Why didn't you contact us?" she said, obviously strained. "Don't you try to find the families?"

We should go, I thought. Now. But Ryan, who had no idea where and how Lucy Edwards had been found—something I was certain from her expression that the sister *did*—said calmly, "I'm so sorry. We're not always able to—"

"We had no idea what had happened to Lucy." Julia Redmond's voice was tighter, speaking over him. "Surely *you people*"—she spat it disdainfully—"can recognize *problems* like Lucy's. Why weren't you watching her? Why wasn't she at your 'shelter' instead of freezing to death on the street?" Her voice was rising, louder and more shrill with each question. "How could you let her die in a pile of garbage?" People were listening, turning to look at the three of us.

Julia Redmond realized it and leaned in close, her face twisted with anger and bitterness. "She came to you for help," she hissed. "And you let her die. You killed her."

It was as if she had spoken to the deepest part of my conscience. Any small bit of assurance I had shattered. "I'm so sorry," I whispered. "We . . . we'll go." I walked toward the door fast, dragging Ryan behind me. I kept my back to the room as we stood at the coat check, praying the girl would move faster, even thinking of leaving without them, and waiting to feel the hard, accusing hand of the sister or brother or any of the other people standing in the room.

"What do you—"

"Shh," I hissed at Ryan. "Not now."

After an eternity, our coats came. I shrugged mine on, hurried Ryan into his, grabbed his hand, and pushed out into the freezing night.

"What on earth just happened?" Ryan asked, turning to face me on the porch as the door shushed closed behind us. "Why was that lady—"

"Well, isn't this cute?"

I can't even pinpoint the feelings that flooded me—relief, anxiety, longing, fear—at hearing Zander's voice. He stepped out of the shadows, where he'd been leaning, into the dim light from the front door.

"You kids have fun in there?" he asked lightly.

"Who the hell are you?" Ryan's hand tightened on mine.

Zander looked at me meaningfully. "Would you like to intro-duce us, Cassandra?"

I swallowed hard. Could this get any more awkward? "Zan-der, this is Ryan. We work together. Ryan"—I glanced from one to the other—"this is Zander. We go to school together."

Ryan looked at me, waiting for more of an explanation proba-bly, but I turned to Zander instead. "What are you doing here?"

"I came to keep you company." He walked closer, his eyes hold-ing mine as he added more softly, "And to stop you from doing what you just did."

I looked down, feeling the awfulness of facing Julia Redmond all over again.

Zander shook his head sadly. "What purpose did that serve, Cassie?" He waited a second, then reached out and gently put his hand under my chin, raising my face to his, oblivious to Ryan standing there, still holding my hand. "None, right?"

I felt the pinprick of tears. "Worse than none," I whispered.

He nodded slowly, his lips pursed.

"Cassie?" Ryan asked, finally letting go of my hand and cross-ing his arms. "What exactly is going on here?"

Zander looked at him appraisingly. They stood at roughly the same height, but so different in every other way: Zander broad beside Ryan's lankiness, dark to Ryan's light. "Nothing that con-cerns you," Zander answered.

Ryan shot him a glare, then looked back at me. "Cassie?"

"It's okay, Ryan," I said tiredly. "I can't really explain, but Zan-der's right. You don't need to worry about it."

"Well, I think we should head out. Are you ready?"

I knew Ryan already knew the answer. The way he looked from me to Zander told me he'd figured it out: I was leaving with this guy, whoever he was. I sighed, feeling like the world's biggest jerk, not just for right now, but for all of it. Making him a stand-in for Jack, even if he didn't know it. "I'm sorry, Ryan. I need to talk to Zander. He'll give me a ride home."

Ryan nodded, barely meeting my eyes. "Okay," he said tightly. "Guess I'll see you at work."

"Ryan, hey—" I caught his arm. "Thanks for coming with me."

"Yeah. Sure." He glanced quickly at Zander again, then back at me. "Good luck, Cassie," he said. "With . . . whatever."

Ryan walked to his car without looking back.

After he'd pulled away, tires squealing against the pavement, I spun to face Zander. "Did you follow me here?" I demanded, incensed at the thought of it.

He shook his head. "Didn't need to. I knew you'd come."

"How?"

"Oh, Cassie." Zander sighed, smiling at me and shaking his head. "I can read you like a book." He put on a falsetto. "I found her obituary and she has a family, worked at a bank . . . ," he mimicked, before returning to his normal voice. "You think I couldn't figure out where that would lead?"

I didn't answer.

He rested his hands gently on my shoulders, turning me to look him full in the face. His eyes were almost black, glittering and looking deep into me. I was ready for him to chide me about Lucy Edwards and how foolish I'd been. Instead, he said, "I saw you in there, holding his hand." Zander hesitated. "Does he mean something to you?"

"Jealous?" I asked it lightly, though a secret thrill ran through me.

"No," he said, glancing down and shifting his weight before meeting my eyes again. "I just wish you'd asked me to come with you, not him."

It wasn't his words so much as the way Zander looked—uncertain in a way I'd never seen him look. It was as if he'd chipped away a tiny fragment of his shell to show me there *was* something soft and vulnerable behind it after all. Something capable of being hurt.

He slid his hands down my arms, my skin tingling in their wake despite the layers of coat and clothes between us. He caught both of my hands in his and pulled me close, wrapping my arms around his back, pressing my chest against his.

"You know he can't be for you what I can, Cassie," he murmured, his voice drifting down, words encircling me. "He'll never understand you like I do. You and I, we belong together. We fit."

I felt a bitter saltiness in my throat and my eyes teared so suddenly it caught me unprepared. I'd been a pretty good faker most of my life, but I wasn't sure I'd ever truly *belonged* anywhere. How could I when the most essential thing about me is so strange and secret? So different.

"Zander, with Ryan . . . it's not anything . . ."

"Shh," he said, gently kissing my hair. "I thought I told you to tell him you were taken anyway," he teased. And then Zander pulled me away, holding me at arm's length to see into my eyes, all teasing gone. "But about what you saw in there, Cassie? I want to be sure you understand that we did the right thing."

I thought about it for a long minute, watching Zander's eyes and seeing a flicker of disapproval when I didn't answer right away.

"I'm not sure, Zander," I said finally, trying to be both honest and appeasing. "I'd like to think we did. I can see that there probably wasn't a future for her and that she'd made her bed. But then I think about her sister and all those people in there—they seem like a good family. Like they really cared." I shook my head. "I think mostly I believe it, but . . ."

"But you're not totally sure."

"No. And I wonder if I ever can be."

Zander pursed his lips. I knew he was disappointed and it didn't feel good. "I hope you learn, Cassie," he said, letting go of me, all but the one hand he used to lead me to the car. "Or you're going to have a very hard road."

chapter 24

It was just past eight when Zander dropped me at the apartment. I watched his taillights fade away. On the ride, I'd tried to think about the good things—the way he'd said we belonged together, the thrill of his claiming me that way—but I couldn't shake his disappointment in my uncertainty about Lucy Edwards, and worse—couldn't shake the uncertainty itself. Zander was what I'd been looking for, a guide for this strange power. So why did I have such a hard time trusting him? Even in the face of the most obvious of marked people like Lucy Edwards?

Why—if I belonged the way he said I did—did I still feel alone?

Maybe because the only thing connecting us was our morbid abilities. And a physical attraction. Nothing more. Nothing *real*. He'd never asked what I was like as a kid or what I did at the holidays or how I celebrated my last birthday. He didn't know what I hoped to do or be next year or ten years from now. And he hadn't volunteered any of that about himself either.

After all the stuff that had happened this week, what I really wanted—yearned for—was someone who could tell me it would be okay. That whatever I saw and whatever I decided, *I'd* be okay. Someone who knew me well enough for that to be believable.

I opened my phone before I chickened out, my hands shaking as I pressed buttons, scrolling through my contacts for the one I needed. The one I'd pulled up a hundred times since leaving Pennsylvania but never mustered the courage to call. It had been easier to fool myself with texts.

I had so many memories of Jack scattered across the years; like happier counterpoints to the mark. I've replayed them like favorite songs, sometimes imagining I could feel the scratchiness of his wool sweater against my cheek or smell the smoke from his living room fireplace.

I'd spent almost every Sunday with him and his mom before I left, snuggled against Jack's chest while the three of us watched a movie or sprawled on the living room floor around a game of Monopoly. I was still living in the apartment where I'd grown up, the one I'd shared with Nan. But it was stripped of personality, most of our things packed, though I hadn't been sure for what. It felt bland and impersonal, no longer like a home. Not like Jack's house.

"I'm glad you're spending so much time with us, Cassie," Jack's mom said one Sunday while we worked in the kitchen together. It was mid-October and we were cutting apples from a bag her neighbor had dropped off and tossing them in a pot of simmering water.

"Thanks, Mrs. P.," I answered, smiling. "I am too."

"It's been a tough couple months for you."

I nodded. Jack's mom had come to Nan's funeral, like most of my classmates and their parents. But she'd actually known Nan, having lived so close to us back when Jack and I were kids.

"You seem like you're in a good place now."

"I am, mostly," I said, adding with a smile, "Always, when I'm here."

She smiled back. "It's good to see Jack with you. I'd always hoped . . ." She stopped, a little embarrassed. "What I mean to say is that he seems very happy, too."

We ate dinner later, sat by the fire, the smell of cinnamon and apples crisp like fall. His mom went to bed around nine.

"Early shift tomorrow," she said, heading for the stairs and giving us a wave and a wink. "Be good."

Jack and I lay on the sofa, not talking, totally content. I felt so small—my just-over five-feet beside his just-under six. Upstairs we heard the water run, toilet flush, doors close.

It was so warm and comfortable I must have dozed. The next time I looked at the clock, it was after ten.

"I should go," I said, sitting up lazily and looking at the dark windowpanes. "Walk me home?"

"No."

I smiled, still staring at the cold outdoors. "C'mon, sleepyhead, before we're too tired." I turned to face him.

Jack shook his head, reached for my hand. "Stay with me."

"Oh, Jack, I'd love to, but your mom—"

"What about her?" he interrupted. "She loves having you here. She loves you." He paused, searching my face, then said it. So softly. "*I* love you."

Everything stopped. My breath caught, trapped somewhere between my throat and my chest where there was an ache so sudden and sharp. No one had ever said that to me. Except Nan. And I'd never said it to anyone except her. When she was gone, it had hurt so much some days I couldn't function.

"Jack . . ." It was all I could squeeze out, the rush of too many feelings, too much knowledge making more impossible.

Jack must have seen it. He leaned over, kissed the top of my head. "It's okay, Cass," he said, unconditional as always. "Just stay."

So I did, balanced between happiness and apprehension, almost wanting not to sleep just so I could feel him beside me all night.

It's the best day I can remember.

I could picture the phone in his house, ringing now as I stood on the sidewalk outside my apartment on a freezing March night, very far from that day.

"Hello?"

The sound of his voice—his actual voice, not the one that played in my memories, but the real him, right now—paralyzed me. I could barely breathe.

"Hello?"

"Jack?" My own voice sounded totally unnatural.

"Who is . . ." He stopped. "Cassie?"

"Yeah." I laughed, trying for casual. "It's me. How're you doing?"

He paused. The silence was huge. I could hear my heart pounding, everything in me willing him to say something, anything, that would make this okay. "Why are you calling?"

He sounded utterly perplexed. Like we were strangers. "Um . . . I . . ." I'd thought he might be angry or surprised, but not this. So distant it was like I'd imagined the few months we'd had together. And the years and years before. "Just to say hi," I finished lamely.

"Oh." Another pause. "Well. Hi."

My whole body felt weak. I leaned on something, a sign or lamppost. It was like I'd been holding my breath and someone came by and kicked me in the gut. I didn't even feel the sting of tears, they came so quickly. I wiped them with my free hand, but didn't know what to do about my nose. I couldn't sniffle or he'd know I was crying so I just let it run.

All this time I'd been sending these texts and thinking about Jack and refusing to admit how much I hoped—no, *believed*—that when I was ready, we could pick up where we'd left off. His voice, offhand and unyielding at the same time, told me now how completely wrong I'd been.

I tried to pull it together, at least enough to give him an equally casual "hi" or "see ya," but I couldn't. I lowered the phone, watching the screen wink to black when I pressed End.

chapter 25

In some ways it was easier after I locked Jack away. After the phone call I wished I'd never made. Zander and I were a recognized couple at school. I could stop looking for Jack in every Tom, Dick, and Ryan I saw, put my hopes and memories in a tiny box in some dark recess of myself, and just focus on Zander. My boyfriend.

He waited for me at my locker. We held hands. Sometimes he ate lunch with us. It was weird. Not just him at our table—though that was really awkward because of Hannah's crush on him—but pretending to be normal when the thing that bound us was our history—both the ancient ties and the more recent one of having been at that woman's death together. Having helped her die.

We went on dates, mostly to the mall. Of all places. I'd suggested bowling or the city or even the diner where I'd seen Nick Altos's dad with the mark, but somehow we always came back to the mall. Whatever. Zander dressed well and I can't say I really minded seeing him try on clothes, especially because he'd pull me into the room with him any time the clerks weren't looking. It was easy, then, to forget that there were too many people at the

186 · JEN NADOL

mall and hard to keep my hands to myself in that tight space with him half dressed. Sometimes I didn't bother trying.

When Petra was at work, he'd come to the apartment and we'd lie side by side on my bed, ostensibly doing homework. Often doing other stuff, though I always put a limit on how much. I was outrageously attracted to Zander. There's no question I wanted him. But not yet. I knew his deepest secret and he knew mine but—crazy as it sounds—I felt like I didn't know *him*. Not the way I'd known Jack. Or even Lucas, for that matter. I don't think Zander realized how every conversation we had—about friends, books, movies—skated on the most superficial surface.

I'd tried anything and everything I could think of, hoping to capture that feeling of intimacy without being intimate that I'd always had with Jack. Of course, I'd never had to ask what his favorite childhood book was or if he'd had pets growing up. Sometimes Zander would answer those questions. Mostly, he sidestepped anything that scratched too deep. Or just flat out shut me down, like the day we were lying on my bed, ignoring our history homework.

"What happened to your father?" I asked him in the middle of a backrub. My voice was partly muffled by the pillow, but I knew he'd heard because he froze, his thumb digging into my back a little too hard.

"Why are you asking me that now?" he said.

"Well, I—" But he didn't let me finish.

"You're kind of ruining the moment, Cass." He stood up. I felt bad but also frustrated. When was he going to tell me something about how he *felt*? Something that actually touched him?

"I'm just, you know, trying to get to know you, Zander."

"Well, that's not the way to do it," he said bluntly.

*   *   *

A week later—two or so after Lucy Edwards's wake—we were at the mall again, on our usual route past Sears, the bookstore, the pimply kid at the movie theater. A quick recon visit to Abercrombie or Gap, then on to the food court, where we shared a dish of ice cream. Zander liked vanilla, but it was my turn to pick so we had rocky road with Heath bar on top.

He fed me a spoonful, which made me smile, though I felt sort of ridiculous too. Zander seemed to have no internal censor for sappy couples' behavior because he followed it up with a kiss, then another, things heating up a little too fast.

"Shouldn't we be doing this, um, somewhere else?" I asked, disengaging him as best I could.

Zander raised his eyebrows. "Where did you have in mind?"

"I . . . That's not what I meant exactly." I could feel the blush on my cheeks. "I mean, should we really be making out in the middle of the mall?" Just saying it made me squirm. "Let's talk," I said, trying to redirect. "Tell me about . . . your first day of school here. How old were you when you and your mom moved to Bellevue?"

Zander rolled his eyes. "This again? What a *girl* you are, Cassie," he teased, leaning back. "Should we talk about our *feelings*?"

"That's insulting, Zander." It wasn't wrong for me to want to know something about him like a normal girlfriend would. Stuff not about death or fate.

He smiled affectionately. "I'm tempted to see if I can make you angry enough to stomp your feet," Zander said. "But I have an idea. Why don't you come over for dinner this weekend? My mom's been bugging me to bring you. You can ask her all the questions you want, talk about feelings, have a good cry if you like . . . maybe I'll even join in."

"Sure," I said. "That'd be nice." Finally, I thought. Kind of like the dinners I used to have with Jack and his mom.

* * *

Calliope Dasios wasted no time making sure it was unlike any dinner at Jack's.

"Cassandra," she breathed, almost reverently, as she embraced me at the front door. "Welcome. I'm so pleased you and Zander are fulfilling your destinies together."

"Uh . . ."

"Mom," Zander said, grimacing. "Maybe take it down a notch?"

"Did I get carried away?" Calliope's smile was warm and self-deprecating. She linked her arm through mine. "I'm just thrilled you two have found each other. We've been looking for so long."

I heard Zander sigh behind me. I guess even Death isn't immune to parental embarrassment. His mother led me to a velvety armchair in the center of the living room. Zander sat in a matching one across the coffee table from me and Calliope was between, on the couch. She poured us each a glass of water from a pitcher with slices of lemons and limes floating among the ice.

"There was so much I wanted to ask on your last visit," she said, "but Zander told me you didn't know yet. About him." She laughed. "You have no idea how hard it was for me to bite my tongue!"

I smiled back, surprised how comfortable Calliope was—how comfortable she made me—about a topic I was so accustomed to hiding. As if our gifts were not only normal, but good. "I was a little surprised to find out that Zander was who—what—he is."

She nodded. "I want to know everything, Cassandra," she said, leaning forward. "Everything you're willing to share. About how long you've known, how you found out. About your people." She glanced toward Zander and I did too. He nodded, a patient resignation on his face. "It's been years," Calliope continued, looking back at me, "since we've had someone Zander could pair up with. And what a beautiful match the two of you make."

I lowered my eyes, both thrilled and troubled by Calliope's enthusiasm. It was like she was already planning our wedding.

"Mom . . ." Zander couldn't hide his exasperation.

She laughed again, a light, musical sound. "I'm sorry, Cassandra. I don't mean to be overbearing. I'm sure you know how unique your gifts are and how hard it is to find another like yourselves. I'm just so happy for you both. And it must be such a relief for you, on your own before."

"It is," I agreed, feeling it was mostly true. "I've been . . ." Confused? Lonely? Afraid? "It's been hard," I said finally.

"I'm sure," she said sympathetically. "Tell me your story, if you don't mind. I'd love to hear it."

So I did. Starting with how I figured out what the mark meant through my time in Kansas, learning about my mom. Calliope was an attentive listener, leaning forward, rarely taking her eyes off me.

"So your mother saw it, too," Calliope said decisively, refilling my water glass. "What about your grandmother?"

I shrugged, looking down at my hands and feeling the sorrow that still came when I thought about Nan. "I don't really know. She never said anything about it, even when she could see I was trying to figure it out."

"But with your mother having it she must have known at least? Even if she didn't have the gift herself?" Calliope asked it gently, clearly understanding what I was struggling with.

I sighed, looking up. "Yeah. I think so."

She patted my knee, her eyes kind. "We all make mistakes, Cassie. It doesn't mean she loved you any less."

Zander had been listening quietly, but I'd seen him growing increasingly restless. He seized the small break in conversation.

"Mom," he said bluntly, "is there anything we should be doing for, you know, dinner?"

Calliope glanced at the intricately carved clock, then stood, smiling fondly at him. "Hungry?"

"Starving," he said. "And the smell of food is just about driving me crazy."

"It's probably ready. Why don't you and Cassandra set the table and I'll finish it up?"

We talked about more normal things over the lasagna and salad Calliope served. Vacations they'd taken, an eccentric client she was working for, the car she needed to replace. I glanced around the room, the objects on the walls taking on new meaning: a photo of a Greek temple, a framed shard of painted pottery, a tarnished dagger.

"You like them?" Calliope asked.

"Interesting," I said. "Do they have any special meaning?"

"Mementos of Zander's heritage, mostly," she said. "There are no temples to Thanatos. The picture is one of Athena's temples, from our first trip to Greece. That vase fragment"—she pointed at the pottery—"is an ancient depiction of Thanatos."

"And the dagger?"

"One of his tools." She smiled, adding, "A replica, of course. Not the original."

It sent a little shiver up my spine.

After dinner, Zander offered to do the dishes. I asked if I could help, but he shook his head. "I'm making good on my promise: time to talk about you and me and our history and feelings," he teased.

"I'm enjoying it," I said, defiantly cocking an eyebrow at him. "At least your mom tells me something."

"Oh, she'll talk your ear off," he said. "That's actually my strategy. I figure after tonight, you'll never want to hear another word about me."

"Ha-ha."

I settled back into my seat in the living room and Calliope took hers. The occasional clank of dishes from the kitchen was not unlike it had been at Jack's house, he and I nestled on the sofa by the fire while his mom cleaned up. There was something cozy and familiar and comforting about this scene.

"Thank you so much for having me over," I said to Calliope.

"Are you kidding?" she said. "I expect to see you here often, Cassandra. You're far more than a girlfriend." My heart leapt at her calling me that. I wasn't sure I'd ever get tired of hearing or thinking about it. "You're a missing part of our family."

She leaned in then, taking my hand. "I want you to know I really feel for you and understand how conflicted you must be about your past, especially your grandmother." She lowered her voice slightly. "I doubt Zander's shared much about it, but we—especially he—has had his own troubles with his father."

"What happened to him?" I asked, eager to hear what Zander was so unwilling to share. "Where is he?"

"He's dead."

"Oh." I felt terrible, even though this was the answer I'd half expected. "I'm so sorry."

"No need to be, Cassandra," she said evenly. "We all have our time. Immortality is a myth."

"Right," I said wryly. "Just like the Greek gods and goddesses?"

She smiled. "It was years ago, Zander had just turned ten, but he's still working through it. You've probably noticed."

I nodded. "I've asked about him a few times. I guess maybe I shouldn't have."

"No," she said immediately. "On the contrary, perhaps *you* can get him to open up. I think it'd be good for him. I never imagined he'd have such difficulty."

"Mr. Ludwig, the owner of the funeral home where I work, says people don't finish grieving until they start talking about it," I said. "Death is hard for lots of people. Even ones like us, who see an awful lot of it."

"True." Calliope paused, the silence between us comfortable. "He's always been so strong and decisive about his duty. Even as a little boy. I never imagined his father would affect him so much."

The words rolled over me harmlessly at first, but as I sat there, the meaning of each sank in, one by one, like rocks dropped into my consciousness. Calliope leaned back on the sofa, languidly sipping her tea, looking toward the darkened window. I stared at her, sitting so casually, and played back the sentence in my mind, hoping it would sound different.

"You don't mean . . ." I hesitated. If I was wrong, what would she think of me that I'd even consider it? But if I was right, what would I think of her? Of them? "You don't mean that he had a role in his father's death, do you?"

She turned back to me, a mild frown knitting her brow. "Well, of course, Cassie. What else would I mean?"

We stared at each other, Calliope puzzled and me letting what she'd admitted steep: Zander had been ten years old and not only a witness to his father's death but a part of it.

He came back into the room then, immediately stopping short as if the air were thick with something too heavy to breathe. It felt that way to me. Zander's eyes narrowed, darting from Calliope to me. I felt like crying. Hearing it had put me right back at Nan's bedside the day she died. I'd tried to help until she'd asked me to stop. But the awfulness and—truly—the guilt of that day had never fully left me. I knew why Zander didn't talk about his dad and wanted nothing more than to give him a hug.

"What?" he demanded.

Calliope opened her mouth, but I stood before she could speak. "It's been a long night, Zander. A lot to take in for me. So . . . informative." I smiled weakly, rushing on. "I think I should head home."

He glanced back at his mother, who smiled placidly. "Yeah, okay," he said.

I was quiet in the car, but Zander didn't press for details. Maybe he knew that what had passed between his mother and me was something he didn't want to hear. I was torn about bringing it up. If he'd wanted me to know, he'd have told me himself. But maybe he couldn't, his dad's death the kind of memory buried so deeply it had to be called out.

Zander turned onto my street and pulled up to the curb out front, asking, "Is your roommate home?"

I nodded.

"Bummer." His eyes were dark and mischievous. "I guess I'll have to say good night out here."

My heart raced as he leaned toward me, the way it always did anticipating his touch, but my mind was still caught up in untangling the knot that was Zander, one more thread loosened, waiting for me to tug it free.

"Zander . . ."

He paused, one hand resting on my seat back, the other on the dash. Wariness flickered in his eyes, less than a foot from mine.

I took a deep breath. "Your mom told me about your father. That he died when you were ten."

There was a subtle clenching of his jaw and a fierceness in his gaze that both dared me to go on and warned me not to. Somehow I choked out the question. "Did you . . . ? Were you part of it?"

He let me hang for a minute. A *full* minute—so much longer than it sounds. I saw it tick by on the second hand of my watch, unable to hold his stare. And when he spoke, it wasn't an answer.

"Why are you so desperate to know stuff like this, Cassie? Things that aren't any of your business and can't help you—or me, for that matter? Why is it so hard for you to focus on what matters: *your* duty, *your* history. Not mine."

Zander's voice started quietly but by the end had sharpened into a razor-hard coldness. I felt chastised and sore and a little scared by his intensity, which seemed to be teetering between fury and despair.

"I just want to know you, Zander," I said quietly. "Understand you better."

"I don't need you to know me like that."

That stung. But I tried to ignore it. "I . . . I thought—and your mom did too—that it might help you to talk about it."

He barked out a humorless laugh. "Yeah, okay. Thanks, Dr. Phil." Zander gritted his teeth and sat back, resting his head against the seat and running his hands through those lush curls, his eyes closed. Finally, he exhaled and brought his hands down, gripping the steering wheel tightly.

"You want to know if I had a part in my father's death?" Zander asked, his voice low and even. "Yeah. I did. It's what I do, Cassie. My duty. I helped him go where he belonged. That's not a bad thing, you know."

"It doesn't mean it's easy, Zander," I said hesitantly. "Or that you have to feel good about it all the time." He didn't answer. "Was he your first?"

He looked at me in disbelief, then dropped his eyes. "Yeah," he said finally, without looking up. "He was. My first alone. He'd always done it with me before."

I waited, but he didn't go on. "What happened?" I asked gently. "Did he know it was his day?"

He breathed in, exhaling slowly before answering. "I think so," he said. "I knew. I told my mom. I didn't know what else to do. He'd always had the feeling about people at the same times and places I did, but this time he didn't say anything so I didn't know if I was wrong or if . . ."

"If he didn't want you to know?" I finished when Zander didn't continue.

"Yeah." His voice was muffled and he wasn't looking at me.

I didn't ask more. The horror of what had likely happened unfolded like an awful bloom: his mom—enthusiastic advocate of his lineage and role—encouraging or helping or forcing her young son to do what he'd done. Executing his duty on an unwilling father and partner. He'd never quite made peace with it. Or probably with her, for that matter.

I reached over and gently stroked his hair, tucking the long pieces back behind his ear, the way he liked them. I wished I really were Dr. Phil so I'd know how to help Zander sift through his mess of emotions.

Zander looked up and I saw the shine of tears for just a second before he pulled me toward him, his hand firm on the back of my neck, his kiss urgent.

"Come with me," he whispered, his hot breath tickling my ear, making me shiver.

"Where?"

"Anywhere. I don't care. I need you."

I pulled back a little, wanting to see his eyes, but they were unreadable. "Zander . . ." I hesitated, hating to say no, partly because I wanted to go, partly because I believed him. He did need me. And it was thrilling and intoxicating. But it was also a little scary. Each step I took with him felt like walking on quicksand, sinking deeper into a morass that had an inexplicable and dangerous pull.

And then, just as suddenly, he shook his head, flashed an embarrassed little smile. "Forget it," he said.

"I just . . . I'm not sure." I felt terrible—foolish—for not responding when he'd finally done the thing I'd been asking him to: share something real of himself

He held up a hand. "It's okay, Cassie. Really." He smiled again, sheepishly. "Bad timing."

We looked at each other and I felt like maybe I should say something about his father and what he'd told me. But everything sounded way too trite in my head, like it would diminish what had happened and what he'd shared.

Instead I leaned over and gave him a kiss on the cheek, feeling the gentle scrape of his stubble and breathing deep to savor his earthy scent. "Thank you," I whispered.

He smiled, a flicker of something in his expression making me pause for a second. And then it was gone. "See you tomorrow," he said casually.

I walked to the apartment, feeling as I so often did with Zander: confused. One step forward, two back. I thought we'd finally made some headway, but I wasn't completely sure. He'd given me something real, but only because I'd dragged it out of him. Not because he wanted to. And I couldn't rid myself of the way his mom talked about us, how perfectly my ability complemented his. Did he care? Did he *want* to be with me? Or were we were bound like strangers in our own sort of arranged marriage?

I worried that with Zander, I might never really know.

chapter 26

It took a long time to fall asleep that night. I didn't know what to do about Zander, wished so much Calliope were less a proponent of his role and more a mother. She'd clearly thought Nan was wrong not to tell me about the mark. Mostly, I agreed, but I'd had sixteen years of friends and playgrounds and fun because she hadn't. Zander had had death and duty, to be executed no matter who or what was affected. I could only begin to imagine what a twisted mess his psyche was.

When my alarm went off at seven, I dragged myself out of bed wishing I'd had the guts to ignore Mr. Ludwig's call. He left a message while I was at Zander's; they'd gotten a body in, did I want to come help? No. But I owed it to him, having called in my last shift and two others before that.

I made it to the funeral home just after eight and came face-to-face with the last person I wanted to see: Ryan.

"Hi, Cassie." His voice was chilly.

"Hey, Ryan. Are you working today?" Please, God, no.

He shook his head. "I just stopped in to grab a book I left yesterday."

He turned to leave.

"Ryan, listen." I sighed, not wanting to deal with this at all, but knowing if I didn't it would be a thousand times worse the next time I saw him. "I'm sorry about the other night. I didn't realize Zander was going to show up. I hope you're not mad that I stayed. He and I had some . . . well, things we needed to sort out." And still do.

"Is he your boyfriend?"

I shrugged. "Sort of."

"Sort of?" Ryan frowned. "What does that mean?"

"Yes," I admitted, not sure why I hadn't just come out with it in the first place. "He is."

"Uh-huh." Ryan picked up his backpack and slung it over a shoulder. "That's what I thought." He paused by the door. "You know, you could have just told me, Cassie. I get the feeling there's a lot of stuff going on with you that you're not so up front about. Your choice." He shrugged. "But I've never found that a very good way to live."

He disappeared around the corner. I stood there, stung and surprised to feel the start of tears. You are not a bad person, I reassured myself. You're overreacting. Overtired.

Not how I wanted to begin this shift.

I think Mr. Ludwig was kind of surprised I actually showed up. "I'm glad to see you, Cassie."

I nodded, slipping on the lightly powdered gloves I'd need to assist with the body. "Thanks, I'm sorry I'm late and that I've been out lately," I said quickly, busying myself with rearranging the tools. "I haven't been feeling well. And then I had some stuff at school . . ."

"I understand," he said in a way that told me he understood I wasn't being truthful, but was forgiven anyway.

"You do?"

It was his turn to nod. "I think I know part of the reason you've been . . . away." He gestured for a scalpel. I passed it to him and he continued. "You don't need to worry today," he said. "He's already left, but I know that Ryan Wilton has, let's say, an interest in you?" He glanced up, lifting those fine brows.

I blushed and Mr. Ludwig took it as confirmation. "Perhaps that has made you uncomfortable here?"

"It's not Ryan's fault," I said.

"No," he said, bending over the body to slice deftly through skin, "attraction is rarely within our control, especially for the young."

Ugh. I did *not* want to talk about his, but I owed it to Ryan to clear his name. "I didn't mean that," I clarified. "Ryan hasn't done anything wrong and I'm not uncomfortable around him." The last part was a complete lie.

"Well, either way, he's not here today," Mr. Ludwig said. "So you will not have to be comfortable or uncomfortable with him. Only me." He flashed his merry smile.

I watched him concentrating on the body, parting the skin to insert the drain tube. This one was a four-pointer, meaning the embalming had to be done with not just one insertion at the neck but at various spots, usually because of some kind of circulatory problem. Studying the body on the table, I realized that I'd barely looked at it before now. Partly because I was exhausted and distracted by my ugly exchange with Ryan. But I'd carried on a normal conversation with my boss over this naked dead person without even noticing whether it was male or female. That would have been hard to believe two months ago.

"What happened to her?" I asked now.

"Stroke," Mr. Ludwig answered immediately, used to the pattern of my inquiries. I smiled a little, definitely comfortable with him.

Still, I was hesitant to ask the next question, the most important one. I'd never asked before—not him or anyone else—though it had certainly been on my mind with every corpse we'd worked on.

"If you'd had the chance to save her," I said slowly, "but if you saved her, someone else would die in her place—would you? Would you change her fate?"

My heart was pounding, but Mr. Ludwig didn't bat an eye. He didn't ask any of the side-tracking questions about treating illnesses or how you could know something like that or why I wanted to know. Instead, he tackled the question, the exact one I was asking.

"There are many things to think about with what we call fate," he said. "If you can change it, perhaps it isn't really fate after all, is it?"

He adjusted the drain tube, then leaned back. "Part of the Japanese religion, my mother would tell you, is how things in this world and beyond are all interconnected." He smiled. "I will give you an example: a woman milks a cow in a small barn, little more than a shed, early one morning. She leaves—maybe the baby cried or her husband called. Maybe she just has to use the bathroom. The cow knocks over the lantern. A fire starts. It hasn't rained much lately and it's a windy day so it spreads quickly. The local firemen worked late into the night before on another call. They're tired. They get lost trying to find the shed when a neighbor finally calls."

The intercom buzzed, startling us both. Mr. Ludwig crossed to the door, answering it. It was Mr. Wilton, telling him he was leaving.

He returned to his spot by the counter and continued. "The Great Chicago Fire of 1871," he said. "It burned for two days, destroyed four miles of downtown, and killed more than two hundred people."

"Wow."

He nodded. "Where did it go wrong? Who is to blame? Should the woman not have milked her cow? Should she not have answered the call of her family or nature, whatever caused the distraction?"

"No," I said. "She shouldn't have left the lantern with the cow."

"Maybe." Mr. Ludwig nodded. "But would that even have mattered if only it had rained the day before or if someone had looked out their window earlier and noticed the fire?

"And then you look at the aftermath. Rebuilding the city created enormous growth. Arguably, it's *the* event that made Chicago a place of significance. Thousands of jobs were created, families fed. Maybe some were helped out of desperate situations or were able to see doctors when they might otherwise have been without money to do so. Certainly it made life better for generations after. Definitely *saved* lives somewhere along the way."

He leaned down and shut off the machine, its whir dying to a whisper, then silence. Mr. Ludwig's words echoed off the metal table and counters of the prep room.

"My point is that every tragedy creates opportunity. And each death averted closes the door on an alternate possibility. Life has so many variables, good and bad, in every situation." He rubbed his jaw speculatively. "What I mean to say is that I don't think it's possible to answer a question like that, Cassie."

"But . . . what if you have to?"

Mr. Ludwig looked at me carefully, knowing I was pushing this "what if" more than usual, unsure why and thankfully not asking. "Then I think you can only do the best with what you know and can imagine."

"Would you have warned the Great Fire lady not to leave the lantern?"

Mr. Ludwig smiled. "I knew you would ask that. And without giving it more thought than I have right here, my answer is yes. I think I would."

"Why?"

"Because it is the certain versus the assumed but unconfirmed. I *know* two hundred and some people died in the Great Fire. I can *guess* that people were helped by it, but I don't know any specifics—who they were, how many of them, what might have happened to them otherwise. In the absence of that information, I'd have to try to save the ones I knew to be in danger." He gestured to the tanks, ready to switch over the embalming fluid. "May I?"

"Of course."

Mr. Ludwig knelt, unscrewing nozzles and hoses. I watched him absently, my mind traveling back over his words. Did it make sense to save all the certain dead? I didn't think so. Some didn't want to be saved and others shouldn't be. But what about the rest, the Jackson Kennits?

"So even though by saving those two hundred some you're dooming others, you'd still do it since you can't quantify the others?" Because I certainly couldn't quantify them; I would never know who'd been marked because of one I'd saved or who'd lived because I let Jackson Kennit die.

Mr. Ludwig looked up at me speculatively. "Is it *certain* that I'm dooming others?"

"No," I answered slowly. "There's no way to know for sure. You just have to believe it. Or not."

"Faith?"

"Yeah. Exactly."

He nodded. "Then it depends how strong your faith is. In this case, my faith isn't strong enough to let the fire take its course. I'm not sure I believe an equal number would be helped significantly enough to justify the deaths."

I thought about pressing on, asking what he'd do if it were one for one, but there wasn't much point. His phrasing—equal number—was enough, it told me where his reasoning would take him. It was the same place I always wound up—the impossible judgment of whose life was worth more.

So I asked something else instead. "Do you think that woman—the one with the cows—was damned for what she did?"

"Starting the fire?"

"Yes. Because of the people that died. I mean, it was her fault. She left the lantern." I warned them. Or didn't.

Mr. Ludwig shrugged. "Most religions would say that if she repented, she'd be forgiven."

"Yeah . . . I'm not really thinking about religion, I guess. Not in the strict, like, by-the-rules sense. More like . . ." I couldn't quite put my finger on it, but Mr. Ludwig did it for me.

"In her heart? Her own mind and soul?"

"Yes." I nodded. "Exactly."

With some people you can read the workings of their mind on their face, but Mr. Ludwig wasn't like that. He was inscrutable, pursing his thin lips just a little, but otherwise his face remained as smooth and serene as when he was soothing mourners, acting as their calming touchstone. A soul guide of his own sort.

"I think," he said finally, "that her intentions were blameless,

Cassie. Even if the things she did were careless or stupid or even risky, they weren't done with malice. I know you're not asking about religion as a judge, but rather conscience. But I think they use the same sticks to measure: intent and repentance. Could she forgive herself? Did she ever find peace in her heart? I don't know. I hope so. I think she deserved it."

That was as far as I could take the conversation. It wasn't a complete answer, but it was the best I could hope for. It was all that was out there.

chapter 27

I found Zander by his locker first thing Monday morning. We'd texted on Sunday, but he hadn't returned my calls. I knew he needed space so it didn't bother me. Much.

"You have a good day yesterday?" I asked, resting my back against the locker beside his.

Zander pulled a book from the top shelf. "Yeah." He shrugged. "Nothing special, just hung out. You?"

"I worked. We had a new body in."

I waited for the jokes or sarcasm, but Zander was preoccupied, busy with his coat and books.

"I had a nice time Saturday," I said. I fiddled with my backpack's zipper, wondering if I should say anything about the ride home. It felt so huge, hanging between us. "Zander, about—"

He held up a hand, had been waiting for this. "Let's talk about it later, Cassie. Please." His voice was calm but firm.

"Of course." I nodded, kicking myself. This was clearly not the time or place.

Zander smiled. "You free after school?"

* * *

I didn't even protest when Zander suggested the mall, happily surprised he wasn't going to avoid talking about Saturday. Probing his past wouldn't be easy for either of us, but it was just the opening I'd been looking for. I felt closer to him already. So what if I'd started the conversation about his dad? His willingness to continue it told me he really did care about me. And trust me. Enough to open up the fragile parts of himself.

I'd left my gloves in the car and relished the touch of our palms as we walked hand in hand past Sears, toward the theater. I looked for the pimply kid, but he wasn't at the ticket window. On break, I thought briefly, ready to ask Zander if he wanted to see the new movie this weekend. Then I saw him—the pimply kid—and did a double-take, staring as he walked across the color-flecked carpet, waving to a coworker on his way for a soda or fries or a horrible accident.

He had the mark.

Zander must have felt me tense up. He followed my gaze. "So it's today." A satisfied smile spread across his face. "Finally."

It gelled, slowly at first, like metal inching within range of a magnet. Why we'd been coming to the mall so often, always passing the theater. Why he'd been so ready to come today, even if it meant a dreaded conversation.

None of it had been coincidence.

I stared at Zander, accusation all over my face.

"What?" he demanded. Zander glanced at the marked boy innocently. "You mean him?"

"You knew. Every day we came here. It wasn't to buy a shirt or see a movie or go to that new restaurant. It was for him."

Zander nodded. "Yes," he said. "Correct."

I was stunned. "Why didn't you tell me? I thought we were doing this together."

"I wasn't sure I could trust you."

"What? *You* weren't sure you could trust *me?* How can you say that? You're the one who just tricked me into telling you about the mark!"

He turned to face me, hands on his hips. "So if I'd told you his time was close and I needed to know when, you'd have come? Helped?"

"Of course."

"Really, Cassie?" He lifted an eyebrow skeptically. "Are you sure?"

No. Not when I knew what Zander would do without stopping to think or question. I wasn't sure at all.

He nodded, able to read everything on my face and in the silence. "I think we've had this conversation before, Cassie. On our way to that woman in the alley. The one you couldn't get over, even though it was clear there wasn't a person in the world who needed our help more. *That's* why I didn't tell you."

Zander turned sharply on his heel then, a faint squeal of rubber on the tile, ready to go after the boy.

I caught his arm. "What are you doing?" I hissed. "You're not going to—"

"I'm going to follow him, Cassie. Come with me or don't, but I have a job to do."

He pulled his arm free and strode toward the boy. I had no choice but to follow.

In less than a minute we were behind him, just two paces back. He wore baggy gray cargos and a dark tee that hung loose on his bony shoulders. He walked slowly, with a slight limp, pitching to his left side where his heavy boots were unevenly scuffed.

He was going to die today.

It was a jarring thought that I'd never get used to no matter how many times I saw the mark. Zander kept a steady distance behind him, not moving closer, but giving no room for his prey to escape. I stayed right beside Zander, with no idea how to stop him or if I should.

The boy was my age, at most. Had his whole life ahead of him. He could grow up to cure AIDS or be a world leader or business pioneer. Or a school shooter or rapist or drug dealer.

I knew nothing about him and had no time to learn.

He glanced lazily into the stores he passed, totally oblivious to the fact that Death was right behind him. I willed him to stay in the open, give me time to decide. I was sure Zander would need a little privacy or at least a chance to get close to the kid in a way that wouldn't attract attention.

Was this boy's life worth risking—no, say it—*taking* someone else's for?

In the end, it was a Lego that helped me choose. The boy with the mark looked down, startled by the snap of plastic. He'd been peering in his wallet when it happened and when the man leaving the card store bumped into him, it flopped to the ground, cards and slips of paper scattering all around.

Zander stepped forward, but I darted in front of him, kneeling next to the kid.

"Thanks," he said as I pushed some of the money his way. It probably seemed strange that I didn't hand it to him, but I couldn't bring myself to actually touch him, dip my hand within the field of the mark.

"Are you here alone?" I asked, low enough that I hoped Zander wouldn't hear.

The boy narrowed his eyes suspiciously. "Why?"

I could feel Zander behind me, edging closer. I shifted to the left, boxing him out.

"I just..." I floundered for a lie. "I thought I saw you with someone I knew earlier."

"My mom?" He flipped over his wallet and the second picture was of a woman with this boy, maybe a year or two ago. It was just the two of them, a posed portrait like you might get at Sears. Just him and her.

It made me think of the one on Jackson Kennit's nightstand, and that plus the fact that this slouchy, too-cool-looking kid actually kept a picture of his mom in his wallet, was all it took.

"Listen," I said, cutting my eyes to the side, looking for Zander. "You're in danger. Not from me. And I'm not crazy. But I *am* psychic. I don't know what the danger is, I can only warn you to be careful. Have your mom come get you as soon as she can. Don't do anything dangerous today." I looked over my shoulder, ready to face Zander's wrath, but he was nowhere around. "In the meantime, stay in the open, somewhere with people. And keep away from the guy who was with me. He's tall with dark hair, wearing jeans and a black sweater. " I paused, trying to think if there was anything else, not quite able to say "it's going to be okay," without knowing if it was true.

The boy stared at me, his eyes big and round, scared.

Good.

I stood, my knees weak. I was scared too, had no idea how Zander would react, but was pretty sure he wasn't going to be happy. I backed away, the kid still squatting and staring. I turned to walk down the store-lined hall but didn't get two steps before Zander grabbed my arm, pulling me into the restroom corridor nearby.

"What the fuck was that?" he hissed, his hand squeezing too tight.

"You're hurting me!" I pried his fingers off, shaking my arm and wincing. There would be bruises. Beyond him, I could see the kid, gathering the rest of his things, looking left, then right, then back again. Flipping open his phone. Dialing.

Zander followed my gaze. "You think you did him a favor, Cassie? You didn't. He's going to die anyway. Maybe even tomorrow. When I won't be there to help him." Zander's face was flushed with anger, his fists tight. "And what about the other person? The one you killed by saving him? Does it feel good to know you're responsible for that? Does it?" He shook his head, fury clear in his furrowed brow. "Did you feel bad for him because he's just a kid?" He said the last part mockingly, singsong, his face contorted, almost ugly. "You are way too human," he told me again, adding, "and in case you think that's a compliment, let me be clear. It's not."

Zander spun on his heel and walked fiercely away, his footsteps sharp punctuation in the cold tiled hall.

I sagged against the wall, feeling sick. Then, startled by the thought that it wasn't over, that Zander could be going after him right now, I checked on the boy.

The mark was gone. Just like that.

I should have felt elated. There *was* a flat sort of joy, but I couldn't help thinking of what Zander had said about the other person. And worrying that he might still try something, not realizing that already his chance had passed. I darted to the hallway opening, looking left and right for Zander, but he was gone. Maybe he could feel it, too. That the boy's time was no longer today or any day near.

The boy had started walking and, as much for something to do as to protect him, I followed, staying far behind, out of sight. He did exactly as I'd said, keeping out of stores, going directly to the food court, sitting nervously at a table, his back to the wall. Good boy, I thought dully.

I sat too, watching the people pass, half expecting to see the mark having magically jumped to one of them, but of course that would be too convenient. I could imagine it, though. On that lady, pushing a stroller. What would become of her little girl if it were her? Or the man busily talking on his phone, a concerned look on his face. He might be a daddy too, or a son taking care of an elderly mother.

I rested my head in my hands, desperately rubbing my temples. Maybe Zander was right. Maybe I was too human.

I felt, more than saw, the boy stand and I looked up. His mother hurried over and he reached for her, relief making his body sag into her hug, not at all embarrassed at the way she cupped his face, palms on either cheek to stare into his eyes in the middle of the mall. She had a nurse's uniform on, her tag still pinned to her chest. It told me she'd dropped everything when she heard his voice.

She led him carefully to the door. He stayed unmarked even as they pushed out into the frigid and darkening night.

It might have been a full minute or two later that I noticed it, a tiny spark of feeling, warm and fighting for space against the gloom that usually came after seeing the mark. I had done something good. I had saved that boy. I had made that woman's life better, happier. Even more, I sensed that I had kept it livable.

It was impossible to prove or quantify, but deep down in my heart, in my conscience, I knew. I believed.

chapter 28

I texted Jack that night. I thought about it for a long time first, scrolling back over the notes I'd sent him these past months. A string of light, conversational updates, all unanswered. I'd failed him miserably, I knew now. I'd had a chance, more than one, to tell the truth, to open up to him the way I'd wanted Zander to open up to me. The difference was that Jack wasn't someone I'd just met a few months ago. He was part of my childhood, someone I knew was safe. And still I'd held back. Not just my secret, but my feelings. I owed it to him—and to myself—to tell him how I really felt. Just so he would know. Just in case.

"Life is hard. I miss you. I love you. Still."

I pressed Send, my message floating out into the dark blue void of cyberspace.

I dreaded seeing Zander at school on Tuesday, but he wasn't there. I'd thought maybe he'd call or text or come by the apartment, the way he had after Lucy Edwards. Just to be sure I was okay. He didn't. It made me nervous. Scared, if you got right down to it. He was pissed, and it isn't good to have Death angry at you.

I went right home, turning down Liv's offers to come over or go to town.

"C'mon," she said. "I finally have an afternoon free—no work, no tutor . . ." The tutor was the compromise she'd made with her parents to keep the job at TREND, which she loved. "And you're blowing me off?"

"I can't, Liv," I said, too tense to pretend I wasn't. "Soon. I promise."

I jogged home, feeling safe only after I was shut inside, the door tightly locked behind me. Petra gave me a funny look.

"Everything okay?"

"Sure. It's just really cold out there," I said, immediately changing the subject. "How's work?"

"You haven't been in for a while," she said. "You've been a bit . . . distracted? But they're releasing Demetria this week."

"When?"

"Tomorrow."

I had to get special permission to see her because guests were usually barred on release day, but they made an exception for me, Demetria's most faithful visitor.

It took me a minute to adjust to the way she looked. She was in her usual place on the sofa, but her hair was clean and freshly brushed, held neatly by a dark headband. She was wearing a gray sweater set, jeans, and ballet flats. She was prettier than I'd realized, beautiful even, in an innocent and sad-looking way, her eyes downcast, watching her hands. They lay loosely on her lap, palms down, so I couldn't see the marks I knew were there. The bandages were off and the cuts healed, but who knew about Demetria herself. Petra said she still hadn't spoken to her doctors, but had to be released anyway. Her family would just have to watch her carefully and continue intense therapy sessions. It sounded like a shaky prescription for success at best.

I lowered myself gently to a chair, knowing by now that my silence was no less welcome than my speech.

She wasn't like me, didn't see the mark or sense strangers' impending deaths. Her visions were nothing more than a fear of being followed by a guy she somehow knew was beyond the natural realm. Not so crazy, really. Except for the fact that she'd slit her wrists.

"Hi, Demetria," I said finally. "It's me, Cassie."

No response. Why should my final visit be any different?

I sighed. "I just wanted to say good-bye and thanks. You know, for letting me come and talk these past weeks." As if she had a choice. "It's been helpful, I guess."

Across the room, a patient shuffled to the doorway, mumbled something to the nurse, then shuffled out. His gown hung limp and crooked and I was glad that at least I'd gotten to see Demetria out of that pathetic thing. Even though something about the way she looked now tugged at my heart even more. She looked too close to normal for the stuff below the surface, whatever it was. Her doctors called it depression, Petra said. My mother's doctors had thought that too. They weren't wrong, but it was far from the whole story.

"I'm sorry about bringing up all the stuff I did," I told Demetria. "About the mark and my problems." I laughed a little. "That's probably the last thing you needed: having me come here and dump *my* baggage on *you*."

Demetria raised her chin, letting her eyes drift past me, toward the doorway, then the window. I kept up my monologue.

"There are some strange and . . . well, sometimes scary things out there," I told her. "You're not crazy." I wondered if anyone had ever said those words to my mother—even if they weren't wholly true—or if they'd have made any difference.

I'd told Petra I was visiting Demetria to find closure with her. My mother. But not once had I actually looked at Demetria in that light. I tried it now, visualizing my mom sitting where Demetria sat, in this asylum. What might I have said to her if I'd ever gotten the chance? I tried to imagine how her voice had sounded, whether her hands had been soft like Demetria's looked or chapped like Nan's in winter, whether she'd liked to read or dance or sing or cook—but it was no good. Petra was right. This wasn't the way to find connection or closure. It only made me think of my mom mute like Demetria, too sad to talk. Too scared of her burden—the mark—to reenter the world. The way she'd spent the last years of her life.

Closure, if I found it, would be somewhere else. Maybe in finding a way to do what my mom hadn't been able to: live with the mark.

I stood, smoothing the folds of my coat, feeling like I should leave Demetria with some final words. Advice to help her with her visions or the coming baby or just the world in general. But what did I really have to offer? So I just told her, "Be careful. And good luck."

I hitched my bag, ready to walk away, when she stood, so naturally that it startled me, like we were two friends at a normal place, having a normal conversation. She was taller than I was, had to look down to meet my startled eyes, hers totally clear and focused. "Good luck," she said back.

It was a shock to hear her voice, higher and softer than I'd imagined, wispy like a cloud. Or an angel. I was so caught by her having actually spoken that it took a minute to process the words. Good luck. With the strange and scary things? With figuring out the mark? Or was she just parroting my last words to her with no meaning behind them?

"Thanks," I whispered, watching as her eyes drifted away, intent seeming already gone from her consciousness, if it was ever there.

chapter 29

On Friday Zander was still absent and I began to unclench. Just a little. I didn't think he would hurt me, but I wasn't positive. Half of me hoped I'd never see him again, but the other half knew I had to. Otherwise, I'd worry forever about when he'd show up next.

But that didn't mean I was eager to face him.

"Still avoiding Zander?" Liv asked when I insisted we take the back stairs to chem.

"Yeah."

She nodded. "I haven't seen him for days. Looks like he's avoiding you, too."

I found myself looking over my shoulder everywhere. On my walks home, waiting for the bus to work, even at the apartment, sure he'd appear when I was least ready for it. Which, in truth, was always. I didn't think I'd ever be ready.

I was walking down the stairs toward the cafeteria, mindful of the blind corner to my left and the bathroom door ahead, when I noticed Nick Altos ahead of me.

"Nick!" I called.

He turned, smiled. "Hey, Cassie."

I caught up and we walked side by side toward the lunchroom.

"I've been thinking about you," I told him. "How are you?"

"Dealing," he said. "A little better every day."

I nodded.

"It never goes away, though, does it?" Nick already knew the answer so I didn't hesitate to confirm it.

"No, not totally."

"But you learn to live with it," he said. "Live *through* it, right?"

"Yeah," I said, feeling the pang of Nan's absence in the center of my body, not where my heart is exactly, more where I imagined the core of my being existed. Where it was always raw and, I suspected, always would be.

People can learn to live with a lot. Nan had been old, Nick's father had made mistakes, but that boy—the image of his mother holding his face in the food court as if everything around them evaporated when she looked at her only son. The more I pictured it, the more certain I was that I'd done the right thing, that her sadness might have been too huge to get past.

"Hey, Nick?"

"Yeah?"

"What do you think your dad would have done if he'd had more time?" It was a brazen question, but I could see Nick had enough emotional scar tissue and trusted me enough that I could ask it.

"Truthfully? It's probably fifty-fifty. I'd like to believe he'd have stayed clean, kept his job, been a productive member of society, you know? That's how I'm going to try to think of him: go-karting at Lakeland Park instead of the times I found him passed out on the sofa or screaming at my mom when he came to pick me up wasted and she wouldn't let me go." Nick shook his head, his smile forced. "Doesn't sound like I'm doing a very good job of it so far, does it?"

"It's pretty hard to get your feelings sorted out, much less your memories," I said. "They just come as they come."

"Right." Nick passed a hand across his brow. "But honestly, with my dad? It's probably just as likely he'd have been back to drinking by the end of the year. Out of work, on welfare, or worse. History would tell me that's the truth." We'd reached the cafeteria and Nick stopped, clearly not wanting to continue this conversation in the crowd. "But I'm going to try to believe what I want to believe. There's no harm in that, right?"

"None at all."

He nodded and waved to a friend. "I'm going to go catch up with Adam. See ya around?"

"Yeah, see ya."

He was there when I left school, waiting outside the doorway I'd been going out the last few days. The one opposite from where he usually parked. Obviously he'd been watching.

"Get in," Zander called through the open passenger window.

Was he crazy? "No thanks," I called, walking faster. Though every bit of my body screamed at me to run, I fought it. Don't show the predator your fear, right?

I heard his car door slam shut behind me and I turned to face him, folding my arms across my chest.

"You can't avoid me forever, Cassie."

"You're the one who's been avoiding *me*, Zander. I've been at school every day. Haven't seen you there."

"I've been busy."

"At the escort service?"

He smiled. "I like a girl with a sense of humor. Yes, as it happens. And other things."

"You didn't do anything to that boy, did you?" It had occurred to me later, after I'd watched him and his mother walk away with no idea who they were or where they lived, that Zander might keep after him, do something that would leave him fucked up. It had also occurred to me that maybe that's what happened to Demetria, what was wrong with her. "The mark left him, you know," I said. "Right there at the mall. It's not his time anymore. I would have told you, but . . ."

Zander held his hand up wearily. "No, Cassie, I didn't go after your little boy. He's fine."

I was careful to hide my relief, wary of showing Zander how important it was to me. Instead, I asked the other thing that had been weighing on me, "How did you find me, Zander?"

"What do you mean?" He frowned. "I waited outside school. It's become pretty obvious to me that this is where you go during the day."

"No, I don't mean today. I mean, how did you know I was like you?" It was the one thing I hadn't gotten to ask. And one I thought I might need to know in case things with Zander were beyond repair, which seemed pretty likely.

"I sensed you," he said. "You know . . . the way we do."

"No, I don't know. I didn't sense *you*."

"Maybe you just didn't recognize it," he said.

Very possible. "What's it like, this sensing?"

"Like anticipation," Zander said immediately, his eyes gleaming. "A prickle of fear or excitement. My heart speeds up, feels like it's beating harder, there's a nervous, tingly feeling, kind of like . . ." He paused, looking for words.

I thought about the way I'd always felt around him, the magnetic attraction. So powerful. Liv had called him "smokin' hot" so I'd assumed he just had that effect on everyone. "Like being in love?" I said.

The gleam disappeared and he stared at me so hard I wished I could yank the words back into my throat. I thought about maybe offering lust or infatuation instead, but decided just to shut up.

"I wouldn't know," he said finally. "I've never been."

It's a good thing I was over him—mostly—or that might have really stung. Not that I'd have expected him to say he was in love with me or anything, but I wouldn't have expected such a flat, cold denial either.

"Anyway," Zander moved on, "like I was saying before, I've been busy. Attending to others. Maybe the ones you doomed when you decided to save your little boy. Would you like to hear about them?"

"No."

"Let's see," he continued as if I hadn't spoken. "There was the lady at the supermarket. I'm pretty sure she was a mommy, saw a carseat in the back of her minivan. Didn't get that one quite right, I don't think." He shrugged ruefully. "What can you do? Then there was that girl at the park—"

"Stop."

Zander was nodding. "Yeah, I'm pretty sure I nailed that one. The feeling was very strong with her."

"Stop it," I said louder, not even realizing I'd grabbed his arm until he removed my hand, squeezing my wrist in a way that made my fingers numb.

"Oh? You don't want to hear about it? You were so very curious when we first met."

I felt faint and nauseated, but spoke as firmly as I could. "Well, I'm not curious now. I've learned all I need to about you, Zander."

"You think so?" His words were casual, but his voice a notch higher than usual, betraying strain and anger, barely hidden. "We're not finished, Cassie. We're meant to be together. I'll give you a little time. I can see you're still working through some things. But you need me. You might think you don't, but you're wrong."

"I have to go," I said, unable to keep my words from shaking. Just a little, but I knew Zander noticed.

I turned and started walking. Quickly. Hoping he wouldn't follow.

He didn't. Not physically, though I felt him as if he were just behind me, watching. As if he'd always be watching. I wasn't sure I'd ever be rid of him. I didn't need him, but he needed me. And I wasn't sure he'd ever really let me go.

chapter 30

I went to the funeral home, mostly because that's where my feet took me. My brain wasn't capable of thought after dealing with Zander. It just followed the preprogrammed path to my assigned shift.

In the storeroom, I went to work: slicing open the boxes, stacking package after package, crushing down the cardboard for pickup. After four of them my hands stopped shaking.

Meant to be together. That's what Zander had said about us. As much as it scared me, there was a strange part of me that actually still wanted it. Badly. Thinking about him, the heat of him close to me, still made me flush with . . . anticipation, as he'd called it. It would be something special, the ability to share this secret and have the partner that I'd always hoped for. We were a perfect fit: I have a power, he has a power.

But together we are deadly. Literally.

I kept thinking about the way he'd looked when we saw the boy at the mall, when I gave him what he needed to fulfill his role. But he never seemed that interested in helping me fulfill mine. He'd said it was my job to decide when to warn someone, but when I had, he'd been furious.

A real partner would have talked me through the arguments for and against.

A real partner would have listened to my reasons for warning the boy.

My instincts had been right all along. Zander was playing me. But in a way I could never have expected.

I was definitely going to have to go it alone.

I finished the last of the unpacking, crushed down the final box, and closed up the supply room. Glancing out the sidelight windows in the vestibule, I could see the sky had dimmed: dusk but with the purple gray of a snow sky. Another six to twelve inches was predicted tonight, which meant that Petra would likely get stuck at the hospital and I'd better get going before it got ugly. Not that I would get trapped here, but the buses were always late in bad weather and, though I loved the snow, I didn't want to walk all the way home in it.

I crossed to the locker room to drop off Ryan's books. He hadn't been here any of my last few shifts. Or called or texted or left any notes. All of which spoke volumes. I knew I hadn't made it clear enough that I was only looking for friendship with him. It hadn't been clear to *me* until I realized I'd been making him my stand-in for Jack. The guy who was safe. Who cared. The guy I'd known all along Zander *wasn't*: the nice guy. But I'd messed up twice because Ryan wasn't Jack and Jack wasn't mine. Not anymore. Not after I'd lied because the truth was too hard. Too scary. I hadn't given him a chance to show me he could take it. Just like Nan had never given me that chance.

But Ryan? He had nothing to do with any of it. I hoped it wasn't too late to let him be just Ryan instead of pseudo-Jack.

I scribbled a note:

Ryan—

> *Thanks again for the loan. I liked them so much*
> *I bought some of my own. I'm reading the section on*
> *Hinduism now. Maybe we can hit up a few temples when*
> *I'm done or at least go out for Indian some night. I'm*
> *sorry I wasn't up front about Zander, you deserve more.*
> *I'd like to make it up to you. Friends?*

> *Cassie*

It was easier to ask him this way and I did want us to be friends. But I knew how it felt to have your hopes and expectations squashed. I'd have to leave our future up to him.

The snow had started by the time I bundled into my coat, scarf, hat, and gloves. It was still the lightest flakes, like dust, nothingness as soon as it hit the sidewalk.

But by the time I got off the bus the flakes were chunkier, a first layer coating the ground. My footprints followed me the block and a half to the apartment.

I kept my head down most of the way, tucking my nose into the wet warmth of the knit scarf, passing building after building, their insides lit in a way that made me long for my fleece socks and flannel pants.

It wasn't as cold as during my vigil for Jackson Kennit. Looking back, it seems obvious that even then—before I had confirmation that there were others—I'd believed. Maybe even as early as when I'd read the letter's translation or before, when Petra had read me my mother's files, the name Lachesis like an arrow hitting a dead-center bull's-eye.

Realizing that, I felt a little like I'd been running in circles with all my questioning and searching. But I think what I've actually learned is that the only thing that matters is that I have this ability. Nothing more.

I'd hoped there would be guidelines to work within, rules, others who could help me. I'd leaned on the idea of finding out whether saving one dooms another. Crutches, I knew now. All of them crutches.

Mr. Ludwig had said what happens to one affects others—in some ways good, in some ways bad. Just like the Chicago fire. Or, a far less dramatic example, Liv's dad losing his job and her finding a niche at TREND, enough that she'd started looking at college business programs. Her parents were thrilled, though a definite maybe was all she'd admit to. Opportunity from misfortune. Gain from loss. It's part of life, not just the work of the Fates.

Maybe that's why Nan decided to turn her back on the mark and let the chips fall where they may. It was tempting to ignore that people were about to die, learn to be less human, as Zander had advised. But when I pictured the kid at the mall or the twelve marked elementary school kids I'd seen when I was four, I didn't think I could. How Nan had walked away from them, I couldn't imagine. I didn't want to be that cold. I wanted more, even if it hurt.

There were no right answers. The only rules and guidelines I could live with were mine. My own moral code, not Zander's, not something set up by people who lived a gazillion years ago.

That's what I can take on faith.

That's what I'm learning to believe in.

Me.

I paused a few feet from our door, snow swirling around me, landing on my scarf and hat and eyelashes as I fished in my bag for keys.

I didn't see the shadowy movement inside until I had the key in the lock, a figure in the dim corner of the hall, facing me. My throat constricted. Zander. And he'd already seen me. It was too late to escape.

I gritted my teeth and opened the door, aware that the only other person on the street was far down the block. Zander had already had his chance to hurt me, but what if he'd reconsidered? I doubted it. He needed me. He was probably just here to talk. Again.

But it wasn't Zander.

My heart felt like it stopped. I couldn't believe it was really him. I was terrified to take another step, afraid that he'd shimmer like a mirage and disappear. But he was still there, solid and real, when I reached him, tears already in my eyes.

"I'm so glad you're here," I whispered, allowing him to fold me silently into his arms.

"I miss you too," Jack said.

That was all it took to start me crying, the relief of seeing him uncorking all the feelings I'd worked so hard to keep bottled up since leaving and, truthfully, even before.

He held me for a minute or two, then slid his hands gently to my shoulders, pulling back to arm's length to look into my eyes. "My mom's here, too, back at the hotel. She's worried about you and wanted to come, but she understood I needed to see you myself first."

I nodded, the tears still coming, faster than I could wipe them. Jack reached up, brushed away the freshest ones. His touch was so tender, just like the night I'd stayed with him.

"I thought . . . when I called and you . . ."

Jack bit his lip, looked down. He shoved his hands into his pockets, broad shoulders hunching together. "I was angry, Cass. I still am. It'd be a lie to pretend I'm not."

I nodded, my heart feeling like it was being twisted slowly, around and around.

"But that's not the only thing I feel. And a lot of the other stuff is good. Or could be." He lifted his head, meeting my eyes again. Jack hesitated, maybe afraid to ask or wondering if it was even worth it, then said quietly, "Will you come home?"

I wasn't sure if he was asking me if I'd go back to Ashville someday or if he was asking me to go back now. With him. Either way, my answer was the same. "Yes."

He blinked, surprised maybe at how easy that had been, things having not been easy with me most of the times he'd tried. "What have you been doing out here, Cass?"

"Finding myself." Cliché, but utterly true.

"And? Did you?"

I nodded.

He smiled gently, reached up to push a stray wisp of hair from my face; his touch, his gaze, everything about him so different from Zander. Honest, open, sincere. It made him no less magnetic. I could feel the electricity between us, a heat that melds things together rather than blows them apart. The tension of our closeness was the same as the day we'd first kissed in the preserve.

"Jack . . ." I wasn't sure how I was going to say it, but somehow

I needed to know. Not how he felt about me. His being here, having flown all this way, waiting on my doorstep, the look in his eyes—it all told me that.

I needed confirmation of the thing I'd always wondered. If I could tell. Because I needed to. Maybe not right now, but definitely someday.

He stared down at me, his eyes soft though his face was serious, still hurt by how I'd left. Erasing that would take time. "Yeah?"

But there was no way to ask.

What question is there that will get you the real answer to whether you can share the weirdest, scariest, most secret thing about yourself? You have to just know. Have faith.

Standing there with him—remembering the way we'd sat side by side in his living room, both of us teary watching *Bambi*, or how, when we were ten, he'd secretly slip the dollar he'd won from me at poker into my backpack, thinking I needed it, or the way he'd held me after Nan had died, not caring what his girlfriend or anyone else in the world might think if they saw us together like that—flipping through our memories and years, I knew.

I took a deep breath, understanding there was no taking it back and sure—positive, actually—that I wouldn't want to. That with Jack, I wouldn't ever have to.

"Come upstairs with me," I said, slipping my hand in his, feeling the warmth of him, familiar, secure, but still thrilling. Maybe more so because of it. "There's so much I want to tell you."

Everything we shut our eyes to, everything we run away from,
everything we deny, denigrate, or despise, serves to defeat us in the end.
What seems nasty, painful, evil, can become a source of beauty, joy,
and strength, if faced with an open mind. Every moment is a golden
one for him who has the vision to recognize it as such.

—HENRY MILLER

acknowledgments

Thanks are due first and foremost to my editor, Caroline Abbey, for the insightful suggestions that shaped this story and improved the telling of it (look, not a single past perfect in that sentence!). You are truly talented and super nice to boot! I am so appreciative of the entire Bloomsbury Children's team for their support and the terrific work they do in all aspects of turning manuscripts into books.

Thank you to my agents, Jenyone Adams and Jerry Kalajian, for your patience, guidance, and tenacity.

I'm grateful to the earliest readers of *The Vision*, Elisabeth West and Kristy Lynch, for letting me know when I was on the right track. And not.

Many thanks to my family: my parents and sisters—Ann, Anthony, Caitlin, and Noreen Rearden—who are always enthusiastic, willing to read, and eager to hand out bookmarks. (Okay, only Dad did that, but he gave out enough for everyone!) My aunts, uncles, and cousins—Rearden and Bakanowski—who came out in a blizzard to celebrate *The Mark*'s release or read from afar. My

Grampy, Alfred E. Bakanowski, for his persistence with the *Eagle*, and my late Grandmom, Ethel Rearden, for her persistence with Grampy, getting him to read the book in the first place.

Paul Bradley and Josh Alpert were invaluable resources for all things mortuary. And Mark Hall and Steve Lucado gave me the lay of the land in Chicago. Thank you all for your time and expertise.

Without Katarina Dicova, I'd still be writing page three of this book—thank you for all the hours of quiet.

On a larger scale, I want to thank everyone who read *The Mark* and told a friend, blogged about it, dropped me a note, or just enjoyed it and looked forward to this book. I've been surprised and amazed at the generosity of people—book bloggers, friends and acquaintances, old and new—who took the time to say congrats or encourage someone else to read. Thank you.

I owe my sanity in large part to the Tenners, who have been incredibly helpful during debut year and beyond. You are an amazing, funny, awesome, talented, determined group of people that I feel so very fortunate to know and be a part of. Thank you for always being willing to share and encourage.

And, of course, boundless gratitude to my husband, Joe, whose support makes writing and so many other things possible. And to my boys—Joey, Sam, and Jake—who inspire me every day.